DAYS OF THE DEAD

presents

Georgia

A Horror Fanthology

•

Atlanta Georgia
February 7~9, 2020

Edited by
Joe Moe

BLACK BED
SHEET

Days of the Dead presents:
Georgia Screeches
A Horror Fanthology
Atlanta Georgia, February 7-9, 2020
A Black Bed Sheet/Diverse Media Book
January 2020
**Copyright © 2020 by Black Bed Sheet Books/Days of the
Dead/all respective authors & contributors**
All rights reserved.

Days of the Dead conventions are brought to you by Bill Philputt
and sponsored by Big Bang Toys & Collectibles

Cover art by Shawn Langley Illustration
Additional art by Jessica White
Design by Nicholas Grabowsky
and copyright © 2020 Black Bed Sheet Books

ISBN-10: 1-946874-18-3
ISBN-13: 978-1-946874-18-4

Days of the Dead presents

Georgia Screeches

A Horror Fanthology
Atlanta Georgia
February 7-9, 2020

A Black Bed Sheet/Diverse Media Book
Antelope, CA

Short horror stories written by fans for fans

Dedicated to Forrest J Ackerman. A man who never let his own hopes and dreams sway him from helping others realize their own.

●

Special thanks to
Bill Philputt and Brooklyn Ewing

Contents

Forryword

A thunderstorm and some healthy competition inspired a teenaged Mary Wollstonecraft Shelley to conjure the novel *Frankenstein* out of thin, electrified air. A raven named Grip from Charles Dickens' novel *Barnaby Rudge*, inspired Edgar Allen Poe to write his narrative poem, *The Raven*. A stay at a snowy, vacant Stanley hotel a day before Halloween, coaxed a nightmare called *The Shining* out of Stephen King. Serendipity aside, there have also been some very intentional forces of inspiration, which have moved us to write and share our stories with each other. Forrest J Ackerman was one of those forces.

In the 1930s, "Forry" made sure an impoverished teenaged paperboy named Ray Bradbury could afford to attend early Sci-Fi club meetings in Los Angeles where he met many of his contemporaries. In the late 50s, along with publisher James Warren, "Uncle Forry" wrote and edited *Famous Monsters of Filmland* magazine, sharing a spotlight usually reserved for the stars on screen with the movie magicians behind the camera, motivating many monster-loving kids to pursue a creative life themselves. These kids grew up to be Joe Dante, Peter Jackson, Steven Spielberg, Tim Burton, Stephen King, Penn & Teller, Billy Bob Thornton, Gene Simmons, Rick Baker, George Lucas, Elvira, Danny Elfman, Frank Darabont, Guillermo del Toro, Kirk Hammett, John Landis, some of you, me, and more! My hope is that this very anthology may serve to inspire you! Thanks to all of you who submitted your stories. Whether you made it into these pages this time or not, I hope the accomplishment of writing a story was a fulfilling one that will move you to continue to create. We all owe it to ourselves to find our voice. Once we do, it's our responsibility to share that voice with the world. You have a unique story to tell. You have a unique perspective on the stories that others have already told through the ages. You have the ability to magically create a universe using nothing more than your imagination and fingertips upon a keyboard. Keep going!

Thank you for allowing me, Days of the Dead horror conventions and Black Bed Sheet Books the privilege of being your launching pad to fantastic new worlds, epic journeys, harrowing horrors, and the magnificent monsters that make us shudder with glee.

Your grateful pal and editor,
Joe Moe

Gone with the Wind, Back with an Appetite
by Joe Moe

As Scarlet moved among the wounded
The moaning maimed, the writhing soon dead
She looked each soldier in the eye
A last fair grace before they die

She felt a tug upon her hem
and turned, not to admonish them
Perhaps the lack of etiquette
was lost to need of tourniquet?

But what she saw, not corpse nor man,
that grasped her French lace in its hand,
made Scarlet wretch and pale as snow
It chilled her blood, it ceased to flow

Groping at her satin skirt
enrobed in blood, and piss, and dirt,
a crudely amputated arm
that clearly meant to do her harm

She thought to flee, to no avail
The moment for escape had sailed
For all the dead were rising now
No time to ponder why or how

1

The Southern Belle was torn apart
From bonnet to her beating heart
Dreaming of Tara as she succumbed
and thankfully, her senses numbed

She wished her love were with her now
He'd know the whys, the whats, the hows
Yes, Rhett would know why dead men stand,
"Frankly, my dear, they are the damned."

•

Jack Bannister was born and raised in Augusta and, along with his two cats, calls Georgia home. Regarding the genre, Jack believes, *"Fear is an emotion that we all share, whether it be an unexplained feeling or documented phobia, we can connect on that shared feeling and find mutual ground in horror."* It's not surprising that Jack's influences include Sergei Lukyanenko and H.P. Lovecraft. His atmospheric and moody, "The Imposter" visits paranoid themes of loss of identity common to both of his heroes. If it's true that one should write what they love and what they know, it stands to reason that Jack's story would revolve around...a cat.

•

The Imposter
by Jack Bannister

The quivering of his limbs violently brought Victor from slumber, slowly wrapping his arms around his body to try to get some warmth. Blinking, the edge of light from the kitchen cast a bizarre glow across his right eye, as he groaned and reached blindly for the covers. *Why is it so fucking cold in here?* Unable to find his blanket, he pulled himself up in the bed and waited as his eyes adjusted to the shadows of his room. Still groggy, he swung his legs over the bed and half skipped to the bedroom door to shut it. Turning the handle to let it slide into place, he felt icy tugs of wind pulling the nape of his neck as it danced across the skin of his arm. "Yvonne?" he called out. "You home?"

3

It didn't feel that cold earlier, and realizing he was alone in the apartment, Victor opened the door and stepped out into the common room of the apartment. Another shiver brought his attention to the thermostat anchored across the room. Rubbing his arms, he tiptoed across the room, eyeing the registered temperature in the apartment was a frigid thirty-eight degrees. Skimming through the settings, the settings were right, and nothing had changed. Gazing to the ceiling, the dust that needed to be cleaned had taken life as the duct behind it appeared to have air spilling from the slits in the grate. Feeling another gust of chilly air, he turned his attention to see where it was coming from. Rounding the corner, he spotted the door wide open. "I know I locked that…" trailing off, he noticed that one of his cats was parked in front of the door, staring off into the distance.

Hopping the small distance to the door, he bent down and went to pull the cat back inside. He froze as he saw that the feline's hair was standing on edge and her back was slightly arched, eyes locked on some distant image Victor was unable to see in the dark.

"Rian, get back." Ignoring the uneasy feeling that Rian's reaction toward the open door gave him, he pulled her back into the hallway, finally able to shut the door. The cat let out a guttural meow and skittered backwards, low to the floor, eyes fixated on the door and not blinking as she made her way tail first toward the table in the common room. The door closed; relief was almost instant as the cold breeze was cut off from the source. Looking around, he didn't see the other cat.

"Diego?" he called out, glancing around the room. Rian skittered across the floor in front of him, meowing loudly, bumping her back against his shin to garner his attention.

4

Georgia Screeches

"Diego?" He turned around and glanced through the kitchen, scanning above the cupboards to see if he spotted the cat hiding behind any of the bottles that littered the top of the cabinets. Frowning, he went back to his room and flipped the light on, glancing under the bed and then through the closet.

"Diego!?" he called again. Rian hopped on the bed and pawed the air, meowing lightly for attention.

Looking at the time, he noticed the sky was beginning to lighten and turned back around. He peeked under the couches, knowing that the cat couldn't fit under there but checking anyways. He turned around as he heard the door open. "You're up early," Yvonne said.

"The door was open. I know I locked it. And it seems like Diego isn't here," Victor huffed. "I hope he didn't get out; he's not meant to be outside. And it's so cold!"

Yvonne paused for a minute. "How'd the door open?"

Shrugging, Victor ran to his room, shrugged some pants on and grabbed a jacket. "I don't know but it was. Regardless, Diego isn't inside." He walked past Yvonne and headed outside, shivering as the brisk air hit his face. "Diego!" he called.

Clicking his tongue, he headed downstairs, looking around. He didn't see anything moving but heard the rustling of the leaves on the ground. Pulling his jacket closer, he hooked a left down the path to the edge of the building that they lived in. There was a small wooded area that some wild cats usually roamed, and some neighbors left bins during the winter for them to warm up and sleep in. Peering in them, he didn't recognize the tiny eyes peering back up at him from any of the boxes. He walked to the edge of the property and glanced into the denser part of the woods.

5

"Diego!" he called again. Silence greeted him.

Frustrated, he turned around, heading toward the apartment. "Any luck?" Yvonne asked as he entered. She was finishing a cup of coffee and reached to grab her scarf. "I'll go look in a minute. He couldn't have gone far." She made her way out the door.

"Yeah, if he did, I'm sure he'll come back. I don't think he'd have wandered to the street."

Yvonne stepped out the door. "I need to get ready for work." Victor headed back to his room.

Rian was still curled up on his bed as Victor grabbed clothes from the closet and a towel out of the hamper. Turning on the radio, he started the shower to get ready for the day.

***

Diego was on Victor's mind all day. He was distracted at work, creating flyers and posting on social media about the missing feline. A close friend went to the surrounding neighborhoods the first day and rode around for a bit attempting to see if they could spot him. That first day felt so long, but the pit of worry that had engulfed his stomach felt like the weight of the world. Being January, the temperature wasn't going to get any warmer anytime soon, and Diego was very timid. He had never been outdoors before and Victor wasn't sure how he would be able to get food. That first day turned into several. It felt like the same routine – he'd wake up and search outside for the cat, go to work, come home and go search for the cat. Yvonne did the same thing. Those days turned into weeks, and then a month went by. Victor was in tears one evening and made peace with the fact that he would never see the cat again. In his last attempt, he was outside on a Saturday and heard a shriek like a baby screaming. He looked up and noticed a hawk carrying something in its talons.

"I hope that if that happened to Diego, it isn't that long and drawn out." The shrieking stopped when the hawk landed, and Victor went back into the apartment.

Rian tried to keep Victor's spirits up, but he was so saddened by the missing cat, he didn't really know how to act. He wasn't the same. Work was a blur, and his days started to run together. But he knew he couldn't go on forever being down. He finally was ok enough to admit that the cat was never coming back. During the 6th week, he received notice that he needed to be home to pick up a shipment and sign for it, so at lunchtime he mentioned he'd be late getting back to work and headed out. When he got home, the package was just being delivered and he noticed Yvonne eyeing him from the window. As he headed up the stairs, a slinky grey cat came strolling around the bushes from the back of the apartment building.

"Yvonne!" he called up. "Look!"

The cat had the same color as Rian but was noticeably smaller. The cat came a little closer, but as Victor stepped off the landing to go to the animal, the cat jumped up and darted back toward the wooded area. Sprinting after the cat, Victor stopped at the edge of the property, noticing the cat slink its way down the incline toward the storm drain. Hesitating for a split second, he hopped down and edged down the slim path to the drain. He got on his knees and looked in, met with the glare of green eyes that caught the glimmer of light that managed to penetrate that far into the drain. A distant meow could be heard, and he extended his gesture for the cat to come closer.

The cat hesitated, seemed to be interested, but then retreated deeper into the drain. Going as far as he could, Victor stopped as he heard a guttural moan come from within the drain, and he thought he saw a flash of red through the green, but inched further, calling to the cat as he tried to get the feline's attention again. Finally, the cat sauntered to his hand and bumped it with his head. Grabbing the cat, Victor backed out of the drain and stood up in the light, getting a good look. *Same shade of blue and grey, identical yellow eyes that glimmered in the light as Diego.* Victor thought to himself. *Definitely skinnier though.*

"What is all the fuss?" Yvonne came up behind Victor. "Oh my god, is that Diego?" She came over. "He's so small. It can't be." She reached for the cat, but he pulled back. "Let's get him inside and looked at." Holding him tightly, Yvonne walked in front of Victor. He thought he saw another flash of red inside the green of Diego's eyes, but he shook the thought since the sun near blinded them both.

Setting the cat down, Yvonne made her way into the kitchen. Immediately, Rian started hissing, backing away from Diego who was casually walking toward his old friend. The hairs on Rian's tail were standing straight up as he let out a yowl, arching his back and leaping forward, catching Diego in mid stride, tackling him to the carpet. Shocked, Victor didn't immediately respond but then dove in the middle of brawl as Rian slammed Diego into the wall before leaping away, bouncing off the couch and jumping back in without missing a beat, swiping at his face. Victor leaned down and snatched Diego up, and doing so caught the full swing of Rian's strike. Red sprayed the wall as claws separated skin, shredding long streaks from his elbow to nearly his wrist.

"Fuck!" Victor shouted, dropping Diego and pulling his arm close. "Get me a towel!" he yelled over his shoulder to Yvonne who ran back to the kitchen. She tossed the towel from the kitchen and Victor wrapped it around his arm the moment he caught it.

Georgia Screeches

Rian was running around the couch and hopped up on the back of it to gain the advantage of higher ground as Diego ran back to the kitchen. Rian launched off the couch and hooked Diego's left back leg, causing him to spin roll as he crashed into the ground and hit the wall. He let out a howl as he bounced off but escaped Rian's next assault. Victor lunged toward Rian and managed to snatch the scruff of his neck. Lifting him from the ground, Victor met Rian's eye, scowling in disbelief. His arm was leaking blood as it soaked through the towel, and he cautiously held Rian away from his body heading toward his bathroom to and lightly secure the furious animal.

"Are you okay?" Yvonne called from the other room.

Pulling back the towel, Victor winced as he backtracked to the common area. "Yeah I think so. I need to get some alcohol on this and clean it so it doesn't get infected." Shaking his head, Victor continued, "I don't know what that was about. Those two have been together for eight years and have never fought before. I don't understand."

Yvonne shook her head, "I've never even seen them so much as growl at each other even when they're playing. That's the strangest thing I've seen in a long time." Diego was rubbing against Yvonne's leg and purring loudly. "Are you sure it's Diego?"

Meowing, he rolled over onto his back and pawed at Yvonne, half chirping and meowing. "That's what he used to do. He's lost so much weight though. Maybe we should take him to the vet to make sure he's okay?"

Nodding, Victor motioned for another towel as he pulled the blood-soaked one off his arm and set it aside. Diego came up to Victor's leg and started brushing up against his lower calf as if saying thank you for stopping the fight. Heading toward the sink, Victor rolled his arm under the water. "Do we have any bandages?"

9

***

Victor shut his door as he went to get ready for bed. They had to keep the cats separated since Rian kept attacking Diego and hadn't let up in the past few days since his return. The doctor checked him out and he was given the all clear, no issues or diseases, just a little malnourished considering he had been gone a full six weeks.

Looking over to his bed, Diego was curled up in the middle. He was acting strange, clingy and very vocal, where before he was silent most of the time. And there was Rian attacking him, like he didn't recognize him. He had started to fill back out quickly, the weight loss almost erased over the past few days. He just hoped that the two cats would start to get along again. Pulling the covers back, he crawled beneath the sheets.

Diego hopped off the bed and sauntered into the closet. Flicking the light off, Victor rolled on his side and gazed toward the darkness that Diego melted into, feeling a sudden uneasiness. Like he was being watched. A glimmer of red flashed from the darkness causing Victor to rub his eyes. The ink-like abyss seemed to take form as he tried to make Diego out from any other shape, but he couldn't. Reaching for the light, the shadows scattered as he blinked again, Diego was sitting in the middle of the open closet, licking his paw. It was as if the size of the shadows receded with the light, but Diego seemed to be unbothered.

Purring, he started back to the bed, as Victor shook his head and shut the light back off. Victor pulled the covers over his head, trying to shut out the shrill purr like roar that kept getting louder. There was an odd feeling of fear as the purring took on an inaudible roar that overwhelmed his senses. Starting to shake, the maddening chorus danced between his ears, causing him to lose focus of the presence in the room.

Victor felt the weight of something much larger than his cat creep onto the sheets, pinning him down under the blanket. The unexpected weight choked the air out of him before he was able to utter a sound; the last thing he saw was the darkness above him that was somehow darker than the rest of the room, he swore he glimpsed a flash of red that he recognized from the eyes of the imposter he had mistaken to be his Diego.

The deafening roar making his head spin as the stench of decay enveloped his nostrils before he was consumed by the dark....

•

Jezibell Anat is an actress, writer, and dancer who moved to Augusta, Georgia, in 2007, from a life in the theater in New York. She is co-creator and organizer of Quickies, the short play festival featuring original scripts by local authors at Augusta's black box theatre, Le Chat Noir. She is involved in throwing the Black Cat Carnival, the setting of her story here, and she's the snake dancer, Regina Serpentina. A horror filmmaker, Jezibell hopes to write and act in more horror movies as well as create more horror dance performances in 2020.

Jezibell anat

•

The Black Derpy Cat
by Jezibell Anat

The Black Cat Carnival at Le Chat Noir is the best Halloween happening in Augusta, Georgia. Le Chat Noir is a blackbox theatre in the heart of downtown, and those folks really know how to throw a party. They transform their alley into a flashy Midway with carnie games, a beer garden, boozy snow cones, a station for gory photo ops, and the motley wooden vardo where the Gypsy King reads tarot cards on the spookiest night of the year.

On the theatre stage, the Carnival presents a sideshow of circus acts and Gothic burlesque, and the costume competition is always fierce. The Carnival spills out into the street, with a DJ booth, an outdoor arena for the fire spinners, and a dance floor. People come from as far away as Athens, Savannah, and even Atlanta. (At least in

12

Augusta they could still find free parking!)

Last year Ross had taken Magnolia there for the first time. She had never been to such a spectacular party before, and she was fascinated by all the costumes and entertainers. She came from a very conservative family that wouldn't even allow her to attend the Trunk and Treat event at church, and when she had met and married Ross, he had introduced her to a vibrant new world of creativity and cosplay.

It had been a balmy Georgia night, and they had dressed in brown leather steampunk fantasy, she in a corset and skirt, he in trousers and vest, both with high boots and goggles on their hats. As they walked in, they recognized many of their friends, including Magnolia's best friend Elena. Garbed as a medieval queen, she was tea dueling with a werewolf.

At the photo booth, Magnolia and Ross had their pictures taken with a machete-wielding clown. Magnolia was petite, with soft brown hair, and the photographer joked that she made the perfect victim. On the other hand, Ross, who had lost an eye in Iraq and was greying prematurely, looked like an ideal villain. Magnolia had shrieked when the stylist wrapped bloody latex around her neck. Ross had laughed, and kissed her, and then asked them to drape a piece of plastic brain on her head to look like it was oozing out from under her hat.

But he was so proud of her when they went into the theatre to see the sideshow. As the opening act, the sinuous snake dancer lifted a five-foot ball python from her basket and coiled him around her torso, causing several audience members to whimper and run out. Magnolia just sat back and enjoyed the show. As a country girl, she was not afraid of any critters, and she could appreciate the skills of the knife thrower, the sword swallower and the dancers and aerialists.

After the sideshow, they strolled through the Midway, passing Elena and her werewolf, and Magnolia was thrilled when a fairy couple asked if they could take her picture. Ross tried his hand at some of the carnival games, trading insults with the barkers.

They thought he would be an easy mark because of his missing eye, but they underestimated his skill. His hand/eye coordination was uncanny, and he never missed at the ring toss. A small crowd gathered to watch him throw, and he easily won the top prize, a derpy cat, a handsewn stuffed black cat with only one eye.

"It's you!" Magnolia gushed when he showed it to her.

"That derpy cat's a big deal around here," Elena explained. She had acted in a few of the plays and was familiar with the theatre. "He's made from the original stage curtains, so he's a piece of local history."

"I love him," Magnolia laughed," and I love you." She held Ross tight in one arm and squeezed the cat in the other.

"This guy's gonna make me super-popular," Ross grinned.

He was right. The horde of zombies, aliens, superheroes, villains, and fantasy characters clamored for pictures of Ross and the derpy cat as he and Magnolia rambled through the Midway, slurping on boozy snow cones. Several people asked if they could buy it. A pirate even offered him five hundred dollars, but Ross turned him down flat.

"Ross, that's an awful lot of money, and I know we could use it," Magnolia whispered, "but I'm really glad you kept him."

"He's a collector's item," Ross declared. "Derpy cats at Halloween are magical. Shall we go and get a tarot reading?"

Georgia Screeches

They turned towards the Gypsy King's vardo, but the line extended past the beer garden, and Magnolia did not want to wait. So they went on to the arena where the fire spinners were reveling in all their smoldering glory, hooping, and whirling their poi, and tossing their staffs. Then to close the night, the couple danced, taking turns dandling the derpy cat, laughing and holding him between them.

They had had so much to celebrate that year, that last Halloween when Ross had been finishing his military service at Fort Gordon and was looking forward to transitioning to civilian life, when they had found their dream house just a few miles outside the city, when their future looked brighter than all the lights on the Midway, until that drunk driver crashed into their car as they were driving home from the carnival.

Somehow Magnolia escaped injury, but Ross was killed immediately, as were all the occupants of the other vehicle. Magnolia had clutched the derpy cat in shock as the ambulances arrived, as the police gathered, as Elena came to drive her home.

The cat watched her solemnly with his singular eye as she made the funeral arrangements, listened to the veiled condolences from her family who had never wanted her to marry Ross, gave her statements to the insurance company, replaced her car, and buried her husband at the insistence of his family, even though Ross had always told her that he wanted to be cremated. Elena and their other friends were there for her, but she refused to go out except for work and errands.

During the following months, she always seemed to be tired. She barely had the energy for her job as a dental receptionist and was usually in bed by ten pm. As the seasons turned, the cat was her constant companion. She often held him when she cried at night, and his faded

15

black fabric became stiff with the salt from her tears.

And then suddenly it was Halloween again, and Elena insisted on bringing her back to the Black Cat Carnival. This year Elena donned full vampire garb with fangs and cloak, but Magnolia had simply wrapped herself up as a ghost in a white sheet. She was only there to honor the memory of her last night with Ross.

Of course she brought her derpy cat, and she was gratified to see that this year's derpy cat was made of a variegated orange and black fabric and had three eyes. Hers was truly a treasure, and she kept him close, not even allowing anyone to take a picture with him.

The evening had started drizzly and cold, and the crowd was late in coming out. It was too damp and windy for the fire spinners, and Magnolia didn't feel like playing games or attending the sideshow with Elena. So she had a few drinks, chatted with some friends at the bar, and was about to head out when she passed the vardo of the Gypsy King. Surprisingly, there was no one waiting in line, so on impulse she ducked inside and placed her tickets on his table.

The interior was hung with gauzy vivid fabric, purples and blacks and yellows. The Gypsy King looked appropriately Eastern European, grizzled and stocky, dressed in a red tunic with gold trim, with a black diklo around his bull neck. "Shuffle the cards and cut them," he said in his vigorous, booming voice.

Magnolia tried to shuffle, but her hands wobbled and she spilled the cards all over the painted floor.

"I'm sorry," she whispered as she reached to pick them up. "I've never had a reading before."

His hand on hers stopped her. "You do not need the cards," the Gypsy King said. "Tell me why you are here."

"I came last year with my husband."

"You did not visit me then, and now he is dead."

"How did you know?"

"Is that not my job?" The Gypsy King gave her a sly smile. "But you have your prize."

"Ross won him for me. And they're not making them like this anymore."

"No. The one constant in life is change."

"I wish I could change it all back. I don't even know who I am anymore."

"He does. He has been the witness to your life for the past year."

"I miss my husband," Magnolia began to cry.

"Of course you do. But you know tonight is Notzhe Smerche, the Night of the Dead, when the dead come forth to walk the land."

"Not-zee Smer-chay?"

"Yes. That is the real origin of Halloween. The Irish call it Samhain. People would dress up to disguise themselves from the spirits so they would not be taken away."

"Do I look like a spirit?"

The Gypsy King chuckled. "Elena might fool them, but you will not. You look like a girl wrapped in a bedsheet. You could at least have cut out some eyeholes."

Magnolia burst into laughter.

"That is better. The weather is clearing up, and the DJ will play your music. Go and dance with your derpy cat like you did last year."

"I don't understand."

"You will, my dear. Now your time is up. I have people waiting."

Magnolia saw that the tarot cards were back in their neat pile on the table, awaiting the next querent. She stepped out of the vardo, past the line that now extended beyond the ring toss. The rain had indeed stopped, and the Midway was full of revelers. Beyond the tents she could see a couple of the fire spinners lighting their fans.

Now she wondered, if she and Ross had waited to see the Gypsy King last year, would he have warned them about that fatal drive? Could they have taken an Uber and made it home unharmed? Had it even been safe for Ross to drive with just one eye?

He saw more with one eye than most people see with two.

She turned around, thinking perhaps the Gypsy King had followed her out, but no one was there. Maybe it was just the opening line from some new Goth song; she heard the dark riffs as the DJ began his carnival mix.

For the first time in a year, she felt like dancing. People were swirling around her, and she realized that the sideshow had ended. Elena trotted towards her giddily.

"It's time to stop mourning and start living!" Elena squealed, "Come on!"

She pulled Magnolia onto the dance floor. The music had a bassy pulse. Magnolia didn't recognize the song, but she hadn't been paying attention to recent music. The sound had a hypnotic flow, and she found herself oscillating in response. She pulled out the derpy cat, gazing at him as she remembered dancing with Ross last year, and his eye glowed red. Was it Ross' eye, or the cat's?

The cat felt warm and soft in her hands, expanding with the energy of the crowd and the movement, pulling her to the edge of the dance floor, towards the arena where the fire performers were in the midst of their act. Their section was blocked off with caution tape, and Magnolia stopped dancing to watch, holding the derpy cat up so he could see too.

The next fire dancer leaped out, lit his staff, spun it

18

over his head and around his body and then tossed it high in the air. He pirouetted but missed the catch. The blazing staff fell past him onto the pavement and rolled towards Magnolia. No one ever knew if the derpy cat just flew out of her hands or if she threw him, but the cat suddenly twirled through the air and landed in the flames, his black fabric curling up high, waving like a plume.

Before the safeties could extinguish the blaze, Magnolia slipped in under the caution tape. She reached into the fire for the cat, and vanished. The crowd was quiet for a moment, then exploded with applause. The safeties put out the fire as the spinners looked at each other, and then, with perfect theatrical aplomb, the whole troupe stepped forward and took a bow.

There were many conversations about what had really happened there, but even the videos the spectators had taken provided no clues. The Gypsy King remained silent. But, of course, everyone knows that the *Black Cat Carnival at Le Chat Noir* is the best Halloween happening in Augusta.

•

Fingernails is based on a true story Allen Alberson experienced, a day after Christmas. It was fresh on his mind when this anthology was announced, and written in a day. Allen was born and raised in the hills of North Mississippi and transplanted to Mobile, Alabama where he lives and works today. Allen fell in love with horror at an early age, watching old Universal Horror classics on late-night TV. Those films still influence and guide him and were some of the happiest memories Allen has with his dad.

•

Fingernails
by Allen Alberson

It was early when Maude pulled into the Peachtree shopping center. The parking lot was mostly empty, if by mostly you meant empty other than Maude's Chevy Cruz. She glanced at the alarm clock set into the center of her dash 07:10.

"Well now, this is ridiculous," she thought. Looking up at the CVS Pharmacy. "7 o'clock and they are still closed. Mercy."

Then she remembered it was the day after Christmas. They must be opening late. This just wouldn't do. She had plans. A road trip. She couldn't dally here all day. Her grandchildren were waiting. But she couldn't leave without her blood pressure medicine either. There was no way she could be around her daughter Claire and her illiberal husband Jason without her blood pressure meds. No Sir.

20

Not unless they wanted her to just drop dead right there in front of the grandkids.

Just thinking about "him" made her blood boil. Her son in law Jason was such a know it all. Always talking about white privilege, like he wasn't just as white as she was! Maude's dear Daddy had actually gone to hear Dr. Martin Luther King speak once. He'd fought in WWII against the Nazis, and came home to help black people fight for their Civil rights. Dear old Jason had never bothered joining the military at all, and he dared talk about privilege?

"Now calm down Maude," she told herself. "You have to put up with him all weekend. Getting mad when he's still four hours away isn't going to help" But she was already stirred up. "Like a chicken in a fryin' pan," her late husband Lum would have said, and her blood pressure was up. She would just have to wait...and calm down. Maude glanced down at her watch. 7:13. Well, great. Only 3 minutes have passed and I've lost my temper. She glanced at the car clock. 7:15. Well, that's a little better.

She glanced back at the store. "It's going to be at least 45 minutes before they open…" she thought. "Maybe I should go back home?" Looking around, seeing the lack of cars, including employees, "45 minutes may be overly optimistic." "I can't sit here till 9. I can't," she thought. She turned, looking over her shoulders. The local McDonald's was several blocks down the street. She didn't relish driving back the way she'd come from anymore than she liked the idea of sitting here.

Maude twisted in her seat. Nervous. Irritated. She sighed deeply, then relaxed in the seat. An idea hit her. There's a coffee and doughnut place in this shopping center. "I'll just drive down, grab a glazed doughnut and wait for the pharmacy to open. Maybe I'll grab two."

She put her key in the ignition, and just before she

turned it, sparking the Cruz to life, she stopped. She looked down the row of buildings in the mall. "It isn't that far." She thinks, she could just walk it. It would save gas, and kill a little more time. She looked back at the CVS. "I've got more than enough time to waste."

Opening the door, Maude stepped out into the chill morning air. "It's not so bad." She pulled her coat tighter around her, shivering. "Not so bad," she thought again.

She looked back at the car, so warm inside, but she'd already committed. "The walk will be good for you. Just do it," she said out loud. With a huff she started walking.

She headed directly to the sidewalk outside of the CVS. Once there, the row of buildings would help shield her from the wind and cold. "It's not really that far," she told herself, and she can use the workout. Dr. Palantio has been on her about losing weight. This will give her something to tell him, something to make him shut the fuck up. "Oh dear, where did that language come from?" she whispered. It's so vulgar to curse - even in your mind.

The sidewalk was near. Clean and empty, waiting for the rush of after-holiday shoppers to push in later in the day. Almost there. Almost…

She reached the sidewalk and stepped up with a huff. "Maybe Dr. Palantio is right. Maybe I do need to exercise more." The thought seems to annoy her. "Or maybe he needs to just shut his wop mouth." There it was again. Another foul word. Or maybe "wop" wasn't a bad word. She couldn't keep up with all the new words that offended people. "Maybe I'll ask Jason," she smiled at the thought. Oh, how it would set him off. But no, she wouldn't give him the satisfaction. Even though it would be heavenly to watch his mouth twist up as he bit his tongue. But she wouldn't do it. For Claire's sake.

She turned down the sidewalk. "Not very far," she

thought again. CVS, Big Lots, a silly little bar & grill with a fish man on the door, a pizza place, and the doughnut shop." Or was the doughnut shop between the bar and the pizza place? Maude didn't remember. It wasn't far, and it really didn't matter anyway.

As she walked on, she noticed something up ahead. Just one store down, not far at all. Under the large awl of the Big Lots. There was a shopping cart, and it wasn't empty either! It was piled high with what appeared to be sheets and bedding. Funny they should leave a cart out all night. Maybe they were open already. Yes, that's surely what was going on. An early shopper.

The cart just sat there. No early morning buyer pushing it to their car, or Christmas reveler bringing unwanted bedding back to return. There was another cart. Then movement.

That's when Maude saw the woman. Short, hunched over, black. She was digging through a small trash can. Obviously homeless.

Maude wasn't used to seeing homeless people on the streets of Peachtree. Or blacks, for that matter. She twisted up her lips. That sounded so racist. Jason would "tsk" her if he knew she'd thought that.

Of course there were black people in Peachtree. Good black people. Like Mr. Thompson, who teaches band at the high school, and gives clarinet lessons once a month at the Civic Center. Or that nice couple who lived a few doors down from her. The Ayers. Oh, they were so nice.

No this was different. Nasty blacks that listen to rap music and wear baggy pants. Was there any real shock they become homeless? Ugh. President Trump should build a wall around Atlanta. Every day more of its wickedness was leaking out to the good areas around the rotten core. It just didn't seem fair. It wasn't fair. She donated to them all the time. Why not get a home and pay your rent.

Maude reached into her purse as she walked, searching for change, just knowing she would be asked for some. Her cupboard was bare. That's OK, just make a wide angle around her. "If she sees me and asks for change, I'll ignore her. She should be used to being ignored."

As Maude approached, she walked away from the building, back into the parking lot, unprotected from the December wind. She kept her eyes on the stranger, cautiously, "What is she doing?" Maude saw the woman reach down into a pile of garbage. When she drew her hand back, she was holding something. It looked like a toy with dangling legs. No, it looked like a toy octopus. Strange, but it is Christmas, well yesterday was. Kids nowadays like all these weird toys from Youtube and Minecraft.

Maude's phone buzzed in her purse. She pulled it out. Claire. She clicked on the text message.

Claire: [Hey Mom, when are you headed out?]

Maude: [Soon. Waiting on the pharmacy to open]

When she finished and looked up, the vagrant had her arms stuffed into another pile of trash. Maude screwed up her face, "Dear Jesus what won't they touch?" She continued along, her curiosity forcing quick glances., She felt an almost uncontrollable urge to see the vagrant's face. At this point Maude wasn't even sure if "it" was a man or woman. Were you ever sure anymore? She "tsked" and shook her head at the thought and continued on.

When Maude was far enough away, for safety, she veered back in, past the fishy little bar and grill. She wrinkled her nose, as the wind brought a whiff of old seafood to her. It smelled like rotten calamari. They should do a better job with their trash. Then she was there. Success! The doughnut shop.

Maude grabbed the door handle and pulled. It didn't open. She pulled harder. She was prepared to spew a flood of curses that would curl Jason's hair. Then she noticed the small sign:

Closed until January 3rd. MERRY CHRISTMAS and HAPPY HOLIDAYS

"Jesus wept."

All this walk and no candy-coated glazed goodness, Oh well, she needed the walk. She stood for a second and then turned back, absent-mindedly sticking to the sidewalk.

"I really did want a doughnut." Past the Bar & Grill, which didn't seem as fishy smelling this time, and on toward the Big Lots. Just as the homeless person came into sight, the scent assaulted her again. She wrinkled her nose in disgust. Maybe the wretched being had been digging in the grill's garbage. "What won't they stick their hands into?"

Maude was alongside her now, at a healthy but respectful distance. Convinced that at any moment she would turn, take notice and begin to beg.

Then she saw it. The woman's hand. Her left hand, the one she had seen sticking into the garbage and pulling out the toy with gangly legs. It wasn't a toy in her hand.

The realization that something was wrong, stopped her. Something more seriously wrong than a homeless person in the nice streets of Buckhead. "Nails," she thought, "they have to be long overgrown nails, like from a sideshow." Maude had seen similar overgrown nails on Donahue. Or was it Maury? She couldn't remember. Of course, the poor dredge hadn't taken proper care of her nails and they had surpassed the societal norm.

Maude started to walk again, but couldn't stop glancing back. There seemed to be an itch in her head.

The homeless woman's hand kept moving in and out of the trash. Maude began to realize they couldn't be fingernails. They were her fingers. The fingers were stiff, poor deformed creature. That was why she was having problems using her hand. A small mote of pity began to form in Maude's soul for the poor creature.

Then the homeless woman's finger moved. Not like you would expect a deformed digit to move. Not stiff, no. It...slithered. It bent backwards and upwards where as if there was no joint to support the movement. This was not right and Maude's brain struggled to digest what it had seen. She started walking again, and realized she was hearing words. Words she couldn't understand. The homeless person was talking, muttering. Was that a language? It wasn't English.

A glance backward and Maude saw the fingers again, outstretched, looking stiff for a moment, then squirming again. All of them. Maude broke into a run, slow and cumbersome but a run, nonetheless. She wanted the safety of her car, and she just knew she wouldn't make it. "Was the chanting getting closer. Oh God, please!" Then she was at her car. She fumbled her door open and climbed inside, and jammed the key in the ignition.

Maude dared to look back. The homeless person was still in the same spot. Still going through trash. Maude began to calm down. Her rational mind took over. "It was just a deformity, that's all." A deformity and Maude's overblown, sugar-deprived mind at work. She pulled out her phone and texted her friend Jennifer:

Maude: [You won't believe what I just...]

Maude stopped, hands on keys. The homeless person was walking down the sidewalk. Toward her. Of course Maude's car was several feet away from the sidewalk and the homeless woman would walk right by, at a safe distance...but she was getting closer. Suddenly, Maude felt very alone. "I should leave. I should go."

But she didn't. Instead, she pulled up the camera on her phone and started taking pictures. As the woman got closer Maude could see her deformed left hand. It hung in front of her, the fingers, each well over a foot long, squirming. The right hand was still covered by the large overcoat. She drew closer, parallel to Maude's car and she snapped another picture.

The woman looked at her. She could see her face, younger than she would have imagined. Mid-30s at most. The woman stared at Maude for a few seconds that seemed like an eternity. Then she continued walking.

Maude, felt a sense of shame. She had been caught. She was no better than those thugs who stopped to stare at accident victims. But she was also scared. That was no normal hand. It wasn't a normal deformed hand. It was like a normal hand had been cut off and replaced with an insane pirate hook. Only they were all out of hooks, "Would a squid do, M'lady?"

She brought her phone down quickly. You could see the fingers in the photos. She finished her message to Jennifer and started another one.

Maude: [Hold on. Sending you pics]

She looked back up. The Homeless woman was gone. Where was she? There wasn't enough time for her to vanish, but the sidewalk was vacant.

BZZZT! Maude jumped at the sound of her phone.

Jennifer: [Hey gurl, what's up]

She heard a small bump outside her car and looked up. There she was. On the driver's side now, "How did she..?" Maude reached for her key as the woman grew closer. She fit the key in the ignition and turned.

"Ya' Galluh, Ya Dagon, Ya Galluh!"

As Maude looked up toward the voice, she realized

27

too late that she had left her window down. She screamed as tentacles reached through the window. She screamed again when she saw the yellow eyes of the woman. She continued screaming as the tentacles burrowed into her face with tiny hooked teeth. Her screams cut off as the tentacles wormed their way down her throat. As she died, her last thought was how much she wanted a doughnut.

•

Richard Tanner is the award-winning writer/director of *Room for Rent* and *Once Upon a Nightmare*. He's lived on the southside of Atlanta his entire life. He originally tried his hand at being a writer to make use of his English degree and it was that or become a barista. Shortly after his failed attempt at being the next great American novelist, Richard found himself serving coffee. So, he gave filmmaking a chance. About his love of horror, Richard says, *"I grew up with a mother that would read me Stephen King stories for bedtime and a father that believed quality time was best spent watching black and white monster movies."*

•

Small Towns
by Richard Tanner

A cursory glance would reveal nothing more sinister in the town of Hampton than one drunk man sitting on his porch, singing softly to himself. On the outskirts, just east of Main Street, stands the lone gas station that guards the only entrance and exit into it. Once upon a time it had been new and vibrant, a grand achievement for Earl Pennedly, his life's work. He was the first man to bring an air-conditioned building to Hampton, a feat that has never been topped since.

Now years after Earl's death, the Stop and Go stood only as a shrine to a town's once prosperous future. Occasionally, someone would stop by for a soda or a scratch off, but the only frequent customers were the rats. The paint peeled from the building like bedrock from a quarry; each subsequent layer representing another milestone in history. This white layer was 9/11, this moldy green was Vietnam, this sickening yellow was the day Earl killed himself

The building threatened to collapse at every strong wind, the whole town did, but something made it trudge on. Downtown held what little wealth the people had. City Hall was a retrofitted bank that went under in the mid-eighties. The drive through still existed and it was used to pay any bills or taxes that the city demanded. Even in the country people were too busy, or lazy, to get out of a car.

The police station used to be the old train depot, the train still ran by but it never stopped in Hampton, the conductors simply used it was a landmark to know if they were on schedule.

Main Street housed three restaurants and a few boutiques. It was an ideal bohemian paradise for someone who would have read about it in a seventies Playboy article. There was a sushi bar that served dollar sushi and stayed in business only because they served Bud.

The Chinese joint two doors down, called Hong Kong Star, was owned by the same family that owned The Sushi Bar. This made them Hampton royalty and the only "ethnic" folks to settle there. They were from Korea but everyone called them Chinese...or something a little more colorful.

The other restaurant, the one that always had at least two men at the bar no matter the time of day was "Uncle Sam's." It was a dive. One dirt floor shy of a white trash dream. Every chair looked as if it were a hand - me down from another failed restaurant. The pictures adorning the walls were yellowed with age or grease and the entire place smelled of cigarettes. It was a smell that would never fade.

A reminder of how things used to be.

Main Street also played home to two competing beauty shops. The Hair Barn, that catered to the blue haired old women and the few remaining aristocratic southerners and New Vision Styles who tried their best to be modern. The pseudo-hip sensibility mashed up perfectly with the town's.

The other store fronts were offices to the elite of Hampton; one accountant, one optometrist and Jonathan Ackerman.

Jonathan Ackerman was always a peculiar fellow, often prone to walks at night and muttering to himself. Anyone headed home in the early hours of the morning would see his office light burning alone between the shadows of Main Street and often they would see him, his sickly pale skin and too big eyes glowing in the moonlight as he stood at his door debating some great issue with no one at all.

The people of Hampton also found him odd because no one was entirely sure what he did for a living. He had no clients from town and never left to attend appointments elsewhere. The only things that folks were sure of was that in Town Planning and Codes, Jonathan Ackerman's office was listed as "Business: Consultant."

When Ackerman started leaving town every other day it was the talk of the town. The old ladies of The Hair Barn were so happy he got a client big enough to keep him busy, while the ladies at New Vision giggled at the possibilities of Ackerman finding a mistress. The rumors brought smiles to almost everyone.

These excursions happened for nearly three weeks until, one night, Ackerman didn't return. No one thought much of it; after all, he always kept odd hours. However, when the next day ended and there was still no sign of him, people began to worry. They checked his house; they checked his office and found nothing. Even Sheriff Owens scoured the recent emergency service logs from neighboring towns.

A week later, Ackerman was back at his office arguing aloud to no one or himself. It was hard to be sure which. He had apparently arrived in the middle of the night. No one saw him come back, but they were relieved he was safe.

Ackerman received a flood of visitors and well-wishers that morning. Everyone wanted him to know they saw him as one of their own and they were so worried. They all left his office whispering the same thing, that Jonathan Ackerman looked horrible. He was unshaven and unkempt with blood shot eyes, slightly too big for his head. He looked as if he hadn't seen sleep in years. And the smell! The town would talk of that smell for years to come.

It was a Friday when Sheriff Owens had to officially respond to the complaints. He was a very professional man for inhabiting such a laid-back town. His calls usually consisted of border disputes during lawn care season or a drunk in the winter. The hardest thing he'd seen since elected was a bad case of domestic abuse. Jimmy Evers beat the hell out of his wife, Martha, one night. It was a shock to everyone, but Owens had actually seen the poor girl. Her nose was broken and almost beat completely sideways. There wasn't an inch of skin on her face that wasn't bruised and swollen. She couldn't stand!

She could barely speak. Owens almost killed Jimmy Evers that night.

Owens made it to Ackerman's front walk. The odor was so bad that he found himself pulling out a handkerchief. It was an overpowering smell of mold, decay and something he couldn't quite place. He knocked

32

on the door and waited. The smell was too strong to stay still for long. He knocked again, louder and announced himself, "Mr. Ackerman! It's Sheriff Owens, I'm afraid I'm going to need a moment of your time."

The door opened, revealing Ackerman in a charcoal suit looking as haggard as ever. The smell that flooded from behind him almost caused Owens to vomit. Somehow he held back. His eyes watered but his lunch stayed in its proper place. "Hello, Sheriff. Sorry I didn't hear you right away. I was lost somewhere in my studies for my latest client." Ackerman smiled revealing a few too many teeth.

"Quite alright," said the sheriff through his handkerchief. "But there is an issue we've got to discuss."

"Oh dear, well come in, please." Ackerman stepped sideways and held his hand out gesturing the sheriff to enter.

Owens' eyes went wide. "No! I mean, thank you very much, Mr. Ackerman but out here is fine. This will be quick. I've been receiving a few complaints and now that I'm here I can see they aren't quite unfounded."

Ackerman frowned. "But I don't understand. I've done nothing wrong here. I've been a model citizen of..."

Owens raised his hand. "It's the smell. I've been getting several calls a day about the smell."

Ackerman looked around and sniffed. "What smell?"

"Are you kidding me? The smell that's so bad that I've got to hold this handkerchief to my face just so I can speak to you. You're gonna have to do something about it or the town is gonna make me shut down your office until the uh...situation...is resolved.

Ackerman's wide eyes narrowed as did his smile. "Sheriff, I don't think I can let you do that. My most recent client has offered me a very lucrative deal and shutting down will not be an option." He took a single step forward but there was something in that movement that was so frightening that Owens found himself reaching for his gun.

Ackerman turned and left without waiting for a response. Owens simply stood there, a little too confused to know how to proceed. The smell helped him find an answer and he retreated to his car.

Owens knew that smell. He had smelled it once when he was a kid, when his grandfather died and once again in his second year as sheriff when he found Mrs. Smith dead from a stroke. That smell was death and that scared him more than anything else.

It rained in Hampton that night and anyone driving down Main Street would have seen Jonathan Ackerman arguing violently with the empty air at his office door. As fate saw it, only one car drove by; the old brown sedan of Sheriff Owens. He was headed home when he saw the commotion and despite every screaming warning in his head to keep driving, to get the hell out of Dodge! He stopped. It would prove to be a night that haunted him more than the sight of the battered Martha Evers crumpled on the floor.

Owens stepped out of his car and pulled on his hat. "Mr. Ackerman! What the hell are you doing?"

Ackerman turned, "GO THE FUCK AWAY!" He stepped back into his office, slamming the door, still yelling at the empty room.

Owens stepped up to the door and grabbed the handle. The smell was still there and so was the fear but fear of leaving something or someone dead with the crazed Ackerman was even stronger. He opened the door and stepped in.

The sheriff cautiously looked around at stack of books and saw Ackerman kneeling at his desk. On it was the biggest computer he had ever seen. There were tubes snaking from the monitor and tower to the ceiling and walls. The monitor was big enough to step through and it because obvious that the smell was coming from it.

Ackerman mumbled something and the computer hummed in response. The sheriff stared without breathing, trying to put some of these things together. He took one step closer and slipped on a book, falling to his knee. Ackerman was on top of him before he had a chance to turn his head.

Ackerman thrashed, kicked and scratched, ripping the sheriff's uniform and attacking him like a wild man. When the sheriff tried to restrain him, he yelled an ungodly sound and leaned forward, biting the sheriff's cheek and pulling out a chunk of flesh.

The sheriff screamed, finally able to get Ackerman off of him. He pulled out his gun and fired wildly as Ackerman scrambled back toward him. One shot got him in the leg, the other in his stomach. Ackerman and the sheriff's blood met between them.

Ackerman giggled as if he were a school boy hearing a dirty joke. "YOU SHOT ME!!!"

"Because you bit me!"

"Don't you get it? Don't you get that I know everything now? I don't have time for you, Sheriff!"

"It doesn't matter, Ackerman. You need a lawyer and you need to shut up!"

The computer hissed and started to steam. "My client still needs me; he'll never let me go. I'm sorry Sheriff, but I told you to go away."

As the steam thickened, so did the smell and Owens found himself getting tired. He started coughing and slid to the floor. Everything started to blur. He felt his eyes closing but used all of his will to keep them open. Ackerman was on his knees in front of the computer; his wound had almost stopped bleeding. The computer started shaking and a fire broke out on the desk.

Owens was losing his fight with sleep and dropped his gun, his eyes loosely focused on Ackerman and the computer. The fire was getting bigger and Ackerman was crying. The tubes from the walls started shaking so violently that they were ripped free. The movement caused the monitor and tower to rise safely above the fire. Before Owens went down for the count, he remembered hearing the trains pass by blaring its horn. "It's midnight."

Owens woke up on the street, rain in his face and an EMT by his side. The fire department was able to maintain the fire pretty well but Ackerman's office was as good as gone. Hong Kong Star and The Hair Barn would have a lot of clean up and a few insurance claims but they would be open for business in the morning with a few extra customers hoping to hear a bit of gossip. Everyone wanted to know more.

Owens was admitted to the hospital in the neighboring town and kept overnight for observation. Physically he was fine, a scar on the cheek and some bruises on his legs but otherwise looking no less for the wear.

He never was able to get rid of the odor though. He could still smell it, even years down the road he would find himself spraying Lysol all over the station because he was sure it was there. He also switched to a type writer, leaving any computer work to be done by the deputies. It was an easier transition than he had expected.

The only person in town who knew the truth of the night was Earl Pennedly Jr. He was sitting outside the gas station drinking the private selection that he hid from his wife. He sat on an old vinyl folding chair, yellowed by age, smoke and gas, half asleep and half drunk when the fire started. He didn't move and didn't try to help, the only thing he did was take a swig and grunt when Ackerman dashed by.

Ackerman ran like the mad man he was into the darkness, on the way out of Hampton. He was dragging a jumbled mess of wires, they slithered like snakes behind him. Blood dripped from Ackerman's wound and he stumbled to the ground just in front of Earl. The wires kept moving, wrapping around Ackerman and dragging him into the woods. Earl took a drink as he watched this.

Earl never brought it up. He didn't have any love for Ackerman but on the same note, he never had ill will for him either. Ackerman was just a peculiar fellow but of course some people said that about the Pennedlys as well. Anyway he looked at it, everyone was better off with Ackerman gone. Hampton was a small town with very little to do. A little rumor would do better than a lot of truth because for them, they would always need to know just a little bit more.

•

Wald Jāmz Fälschermann is a retired Funeral Director from Naples, Florida, transplanted to Atlanta in 2019. His previous writings took the form of eulogies and obituaries associated with his job. A closet horror fan for decades, Wald never permitted himself to flaunt his interests for worry his clients might think a horror-loving mortician disrespectful. Today, Wald intends to celebrate his love of the genre and contribute stories to it. Wald looks forward to exploring Georgia and meeting fellow fans. *"I've met enough dead people. I'm ready to meet the living."*

•

I Smell a Screamer

by Wald Jāmz Fälschermann

"What's this for?" Miguel mumbled as he shook the glass jar. Coffee beans rattled against the vented metal lid. It was the kind of shaker jar you'd find filled with red pepper flakes or powdered cheese at a pizza joint. Did anyone call them "pizza joints" anymore? Actually, he called them "pizza parlors," back in the day. He observed the beveled cologne bottles lining the counter and the young girl approaching from behind the display, "Can I help?"

"Yes. What do kids call a pizza restaurant nowadays?" asked Miguel.

The girl regarded him curiously, "Maybe, *pizza place*?"

Miguel pulled a micro-recorder from the breast

pocket of his vintage Hawaiian shirt (orange bird of paradise against purple horizon, set upon turquoise ocean) and pushed "record" in a practiced gesture [click]. The tiny machine's even tinier mic was poised a hair's breadth from his lips. "Pizza place." [click]. The recorder disappeared back into the camouflage of tropical print. "About this shaker jar full of coffee beans?"

She tilted her head, "Are you researching fragrances?"

"What? No, no. I'm a writer."

Her smile dawned. "Really? I think I'm the only one of my friends that still reads books. What do you write?"

Miguel leaned casually on the display case, conspicuously confining thumbs and fingers to the edge of the cool metal frame, careful not to smudge glass. The girl noticed this courtesy, as he'd intended. She'd assume he was being thoughtful, not wanting to make extra Windex-work.

She pressed, "Would I have read anything you've written?"

Miguel scrunched up his face as if diffusing glare from direct sunlight, "Dunno? What do you read?" The girl took a breath a child takes before reciting their Christmas list. Miguel stopped her. "Don't tell me…"

Puzzlement tickled her features. "Don't tell you? Um, OK." She was invested.

"What do kids call this place, here?" Miguel asked.

She was game, "This is Lennox Square or just 'the mall'."

Miguel reached for the recorder. "The entire complex, right?"

"They call this store 'the Nordstrom's'. Like, 'the Macy's'. You know?"

Recorder to lips [click]. "The Nordstrom" [click]. Recorder absorbed back into the shirt.

She beamed. "I read voraciously. I read...everything."

Pretending to be a writer, Miguel listened in earnest, but his mind wandered...drifting to the matte smoothness of the counter girl's cheek. Her warm caramel complexion fanned against a blush of coral, set upon turquoise eyes. Miguel smelled the wall of perfumes conveyed upon radiating waves of heat from her body. A pungent fog, rolling down her chin, across the slope of neck, pooling in the cleft between prominent collar bones, launching off the gentle ramp of breasts and directly into his taut face. He made a show of looking at her nametag for the first time, "Jessica."

"What? Oh, yes. That's me," the girl fumbled over her tongue.

Miguel smiled. "If I had to guess, I'd say you're reading...*Men Court Sorrow* by Remy Sargent?"

"Oh...my...God! Yes! How?" Jessica's lower jaw parked on her chest.

"Never ask a magician how he does his tricks..." (Facebook).

"By the way," she offered, "it's...like a palate cleanser for your nose."

"What is?" Miguel had no clue.

"The coffee beans?" She held the shaker and rattled it rhythmically.

"Oh! Brilliant!" Miguel turned red as a Valentine's candy box. Not because he'd lost track of his initial question about the shaker. Because within all of the calculation, manipulation and contrivance, there was still unexpected enlightenment. Jessica saw Miguel blush. She made a little puzzle of her face, not repellant, but curious.

Jessica demoed, "You smell the coffee beans between each fragrance to neutralize your nose. That helps you experience each scent in its purest form."

Miguel's eyebrows crept up his forehead, "Clever."

Jessica was gaining confidence, "I invented it." Miguel laughed and Jessica laughed at his laughter.

Jessica sighed, "This job hasn't improved my bank account, but it's done wonders for my nose! I can smell Tater Chips at Zaxby's from 2 blocks away. When the wind blows just right, I can smell fertilizer on the Birdfoot Violets at the Botanical Gardens on Piedmont.

"Jessica?"

"Yes...?"

"I'm Troy," (lied Miguel). He was a closer. He didn't get to be a closer by slow-playing his game or by rushing it. "Jessica, it's pretty obvious I'm not from around here and abundantly clear you know your way around Atlanta. Might you find time to show me around?"

Jessica tempered her cordiality to get in touch with her Southern belle decorum, "Oh, I don't know about that, Mr..."

"Troy."

"I don't know, Troy."

Troy gave a theatrical, cobweb-clearing head shake. "Shoot! What am I thinking? A bright young girl dragging a complete stranger, old enough to be her father, around town. I am sorry I even asked it."

Jessica back-pedaled, "No, please Troy. First of all, my father is 65. I'd be surprised if you were 50. Secondly, it never hurts to ask. You've been a gentleman and...I'd be happy to give you a little tour of our proud 'City in a Forest'."

Troy nodded, nearly modestly. Inside he howled like a heartsick Siberian Husky. "Jessica, I will make it worth your while. Maybe an hour at most. I'll happily buy you gas and take you to dinner at The White Bull?"

Jessica's eyes widened, "The White Bull? That Ernest Hemingway-themed restaurant?"

Miguel nodded, "That's it! I have a reservation for 8, but I can push it..."

"It's not too early. It's too expensive!" Jessica half-heartedly protested.

Miguel leaned in, "It's on me. You're helping me research an important project. It's a write off."

Jessica nearly squealed, but caught herself as her manager turned a corner to stare at the odd pair suspiciously. Jessica snatched up a vase-shaped, faceted bottle of Tremor by Gestank/Gesegnet and sprayed. Miguel cringed as the blanketing mist stung his eyes, but knew Jessica was putting on a show for the boss. Miguel took a deep satisfying breath, "I'll take the 8 oz. bottle!"

Jessica gave Miguel a wink of gratitude and fished out a box nearly as fancy as the bottle inside. "That'll be...oh, lord!" Jessica said, mortified, "$178 dollars?"

Miguel didn't balk. "Wrap it up? I like to tear things open."

Jessica and Miguel laughed. The manager smiled, watching Miguel's stack of cash make its way out of his fat wallet into Jessica's hands. Satisfied, the manager continued her rounds.

Jessica relaxed. "Thanks! You don't really have to buy it."

"Of course I do. It's fate. You picked it randomly and it's perfect." Miguel closed his eyes, lifted and sniffed the collar of his shirt. "Intoxicating."

Jessica smiled through her veneer of expertise, "It's the latest. Very masculine. Citrus, clove, cedar, light tobacco undertones...and, you."

"I've heard these smell different on everyone." Miguel spoke through an exhale.

Jessica nodded vigorously, "It's true. Here..." She misted her own arm with the cologne.

Georgia Screeches

Miguel whiffed his collar again. Next, he grabbed the noisy shaker to breathe in the aroma of coffee beans. Finally, he leaned in to sniff Jessica's wrist. "Completely different on you."

"We all have our unique chemistries, Troy." Jessica tilted her head.

Miguel almost forgot to answer to his phony name, "True. You never know what's inside a person unless you really get in there…"

"I'm off at seven," Jessica blurted.

Miguel nodded matter-of-factly, "Seven it is, then."

***

Night finally fell. It had been too easy. Jessica, had gone along without a hiccup. As if Miguel had scripted her part as well as his own. Seduction is boring. Sometimes it was good to slash to the chase. Screaming would be the payoff for Miguel's leg work. Glorious screaming. Lots…soon. In the back of his panel van, Miguel traded his Hawaiian shirt for a charcoal hoodie and strapped on his black web belt stocked with his favorite "tools." Wood-handled, straight-edged and serrated metal implements. Oiled, polished, and tucked into their sheaths. He didn't need anything but his favorite Japanese paring knife, but you can never be too prepared. The Japanese knife was perfect. Handle fit his hand like an ergonomic joystick. Blade just long enough to reach any major artery or organ in a body. Burnished so it didn't give a risky glint in moonlight. Finally, he took a heat-sealed plastic bag of Chloroform-soaked gauze and put it in his back pocket. Insurance against a victim's adrenaline surge, which could be as dangerous as a psychotic prize fighter on PCP. Wonder what the kids call a "prize fighter" nowadays…

***

Jessica punched the time clock. Troy, had gone along without a hiccup. As if Jessica had scripted his part as well

43

as her own. She was excited at the idea of seeing Troy outside of work. She had an odd attraction to him. Not sexual in the least. But he challenged her and it made her feel alive. She was a pretty girl with a brain. Well, she assumed she must be pretty because of the way men reacted to her. She had absolute confidence in her smarts. If anything, she dumbed it down so as not to be intimidating. She'd never felt she was in step with the time she inhabited. She was a trendy but impractical shoe. Fashionable on the outside, but the toe was too narrow and the heel too abrasive to be comfortable on most feet. She hadn't found the right fit. She was an enigma and there was nothing she could do about it but wait for the right guy to discover her. She'd been through so many. Troy may not be a match in any romantic way, but his attention made her feel better about life. She would return the favor by showing him the Jessica that few knew. The real Jessica.

***

6:45. Jessica arrived at the park early, as was her habit. She always wanted people to know she respected their time and took even social meetings seriously. The park was already fairly empty. A couple of stray joggers ran by, one practically being dragged by a large standard Poodle. The dog paused, wagging its pom-pom tail in greeting to Jessica who put her hands in her pockets and leaned toward the dog, "Hi, baby. Who's a pretty pup?" The owner nodded and continued on. The dog quickly ran up ahead of its master. Jessica raised her head, closed her eyes and smelled the ghosts of doggie shampoo, salmon kibble clinging to whiskers, and dog ass. Also, a whiff of slobber and Terrier turd the Poodle must have gobbled up along its run. She laughed to herself. I guess not only dogs sniff butts when they meet. I do too!

44

Georgia Screeches
***

Miguel arrived at the park even earlier. 6:30 to scope out the park and spy on the girl before meeting her. He found a comfortable spot in the wooded area of the park and crouched down to watch Jessica pet a Poodle and laugh to herself. Her voice was so rich. It would sound sublime screaming. He hoped there would be a perfect public place to make this dream come true, but he was prepared to chloroform her and transport her somewhere less risky. Somewhere screams were not alarms. It was always better to execute the plan near the meeting place. There was ample opportunity for maximum surprise and terror. Sometimes when you drugged a person, they came out of it so groggy and sedated. You had to wind them back up to get to the shrieking.

***

7 PM sharp. "Hey, Jessica!" Miguel stepped out from the brush approaching from behind the park bench where the girl sat staring at shadowy ducks sleeping on the glassy surface of the dark pond. She jumped a little, "You scared the...y'all sure are a stealthy one, Troy." Jessica stood up and faced Miguel who instinctively wrapped his car coat tighter, not wanting to expose his utility belt and sinister accoutrement. Jessica mirrored him, reflexively snuggling deeper into her buff wool peacoat. A cold breeze rose off the water. A flash from above her left breast. Miguel squinted in the dark, "What's that pretty thing?"

Jessica held her lapel toward him. "Oh, just a little fairy brooch from my grammy. Been in the family forever."

"It's gorgeous," Miguel commented, not really able to see the pin at all. He covertly reached under his coat, resting his hand on his back pocket containing Chloroform gauze.

Jessica held her arms out in a warmly welcoming

45

gesture, "Come here, Mr. Troy. You're in the Carolinas, now. Hugs are perfectly acceptable away from that blessed perfume counter."

Miguel smiled. This was an unexpected development. She trusted him. Here alone. In a dark park. What a lamb. Miguel moved forward leaning so that Jessica could embrace him without coming in contact with his killing belt.

"Ow! Jesus!" Miguel exclaimed, jumping away and scratching at his chest.

"What is it?" Jessica asked with concern.

"Something stuck me." Miguel was fighting to regain composure. Even if he responded with his Japanese knife, he'd need to keep his cool. Miguel staggered. Jessica caught his arm and lead him to the park bench. "You better sit, Troy."

Miguel was woozy. Blurry. The lights reflected on the pond lifted up like tangible fumes. Jessica stood back watching Miguel fade. The last thing he saw was Jessica pulling on a leather glove before carefully removing her brooch and placing it carefully in a Ziploc bag, which she dropped into her purse. Then...blackness.

***

Miguel awakened to paralysis and a numbing chill. In some kind of shack. He was disoriented but didn't feel afraid because Jessica's face focused into view. "Hey, Jeshica. I think yer gammy's broosh knocked me out." Miguel slurred.

Jessica smiled, "You got me there, hon. A tincture of neurotoxin on a filigreed golden fairy wing goes a long way.

Miguel was weak. He realized he wasn't shaking off the anesthesia. "I wash gonna...I wash sh-posed to make you schream, ya know?"

Georgia Screeches

"I figured" Jessica said, almost regretfully. "One of us was going down." Jessica lifted something elastic with a pair of tongs. She shook her coffee bean jar, Shake, shake. She sniffed the beans deeply and then lowered her nose to the wet tube she stretched toward her with the tongs. Her eyes rolled back in her head and she dropped the slippery tube. She reached down and brought another plump, glistening organ to her nose. Shake, shake. Sniff.

Miguel peered down to find his body splayed from sternum to groin. His innards were strewn like glistening streamers that tumbled from the cavity of his torso. He screamed in abject, gurgling horror before passing out cold again.

Jessica smiled. "Truth be told, I'm in it for the smells, but I appreciate the screams too." Shake, shake. Sniff. "Mmmmm. Ya'll had shrimp and grits for breakfast, didn't you?"

Shake, shake. Sniff.

•

Phillip Lawless says, *"I've lived in Alabama all my life, and every Alabama resident knows that our state is a shrunken, deformed Siamese sister draining precious life force from Georgia."* Working in marketing and promotion for decades. In the corporate world, it often feels like an imagination is a curse, but Phillip's working to make it a positive. He currently resides on the outskirts of Birmingham, with his wife, son and "a worthless feline." He sneaks out for heavy metal shows, independent pro wrestling events and comic book or horror conventions whenever possible.

•

Boogers
by Phillip Lawless

It was tough watching Mom die. Dr. Franklin said three months, but Mom prayed it wouldn't take that long. She took a handful of pills three times a day. They were mostly for comfort because we all knew she would never get better.

It was a good run, and she had no complaints. After 84 years on earth, Martha Miller was still sharp as a tack. But I was sitting in her single-wide trailer and watching her wind down slowly, day by day. Don't get me wrong. I was proud to do it, but it hurt. And once I set her up in front of the TV each day, the wanderlust hit me hard.

Sure, I've got memories around Kingsboro, Georgia: first kiss behind the drug store, riding dirt bikes with Dad, fights in the Dairy Queen parking lot, log trucks running up Highway 27 all damn day. But I never thought I'd come back. Michael Aaron Miller — the day they handed me a high school diploma with my name on it, I ran as fast as I could. I ran straight out of Kingsboro, straight out of Georgia, straight out of the whole damn Bible Belt.

Closed-minded living never sat well with me. I headed up to Wisconsin to study English literature. Damn near broke my dad's heart. Once I got used to the long winters, warm bars and friendly women, I decided to stay up there forever. But the doctor's phone call six weeks back brought all that to an end.

So now I'm back home. And hell, there just ain't much to do around here. Not much that interests me, anyway. Never been one to hunt, and fishing's too damn expensive. Driving an hour to eat at McDonald's seems like a waste of time. Mostly, I've been walking through the woods. If Mom's comfortable, I'll walk miles and miles each day. Hot or cold, rainy or dry — stomping around in Mother Nature sure beats being cooped up in Mom's tiny living room.

***

A week ago, during one of my daily treks, I saw the first one. Even as a kid, I found weird shit in the woods around here — shredded books, broken toys, twisted-up clothes, wads of hair. I never thought much about it. But I had to stop and look at this.

What first caught my eye was the shine of it. The fact that something could still look shiny and slimy that deep in the woods seemed weird to me. There ain't much light for reflecting. Near as I could tell, this thing was about the size of a toddler, but it definitely wasn't human. It wasn't moving or breathing. It was naked, curled up and had an oddly peaceful look.

I knelt closer. The skin was gray with black spots, and the look of it reminded me of a fat garden slug. Its arms

49

and legs were curved, thick and stubby. It had weird hands and feet. Each hand had three fingers, curled and claw-like. No fingernails. The feet were flat and kind of webbed, but not like a frog. No toes at all.

Next, I studied its face. Its eyes and mouth were closed. A round head, no ears, large eyes, a small bump of a nose with open nostrils and a wide mouth with no lips.

After poking it with a stick, talking at it and waiting a bit, I decided to lift an eyelid. Damned if the big dead eye didn't have wobbly pupils like an old goat. Next I lifted its upper lip and saw nothing but dozens of tiny teeth. Multiple rows of sharp, short teeth crowded the top and bottom of the mouth.

I talk to myself a lot in the woods, but that day I only had one thing to say.

"What the fuck?"

***

I didn't see one of the "Boogers" alive until last night. Yeah, boogers is what I call them now. I didn't learn much science when I was chasing girls and going to poetry workshops at college. I have no idea what the boogers are, where they came from, why they're here, but I do know there ain't nothing good about them.

I was walking down by Mulberry Creek. There's a dirty wood shack a few miles from Mom's trailer that I normally tried to avoid. Some kids partied in its abandoned living room. Well, they're probably in their 20s, but they're all kids to me. Every time I'd snuck by before, there'd been hollering and music blaring. Most days they were too busy smoking some cat-piss drug and screaming at each other to notice a middle-aged man walking by the creek.

Last night, the dusty old shack was quiet. More than quiet. Even from 30 yards away, I could see a body lying

Georgia Screeches

in the doorway.

"Hello!" I yelled across the distance. "Anyone in there?"

Birds chirping was the only answer. I slowly walked towards the shed. Every bone in my body was telling me to run the other way. I wish I'd listened.

The person in the doorway was a young woman I'd seen around town. Maybe at the Jiffy Mart. She was lying face down, the top of her body hanging off the single step, her legs still inside the shack's door. She was wearing a t-shirt and skirt, but she wasn't moving. I didn't see any blood on the steps.

I turned on my cellphone's flashlight and prepared to walk inside. I stepped over her legs into the trailer door, and I almost stepped directly on a booger. Its wide mouth was wrapped around her right calf muscle, and it was sucking on her leg as its jaws slowly worked.

When it heard me, its eyes flipped open. I could see the edges of its mouth curl as it watched me, but it didn't detach from the leg. Remembering the dead booger's teeth, I could only imagine what it was doing to the girl's flesh. Ragged little breaths snuck in and out of the booger as its jaws ground harder on the woman's leg.

I probably stared at the booger for 20 seconds waiting on something to happen. When it stayed still and continued sucking, I circled the room with the phone's light. Five other bodies were in the shack, each lifeless and each with a booger attached. A troublemaker everyone in town knew, Randy Wright, sat shirtless on a ripped chair. A slimy booger was snuggled up on his side, sucking and chewing on the skin between his ribs and hip. Janice Wilkins, a woman that I met at Mom's church, was on the floor propped up in a corner. She had a booger in her lap latched onto the back of her left hand. The booger bit or sucked with such force that her fingers were spread wide

51

and looked to be bending backwards towards the booger's face. The angle of the fingers made me feel sick.

I took a quick inventory of the other bodies — two men, one woman. They all had boogers attached. The woman was face down on the floor and her skirt was pulled down around her ankles. A booger was working on the inside of her left thigh. The men were sitting on the couch. Both wore only their underwear, and each had two boogers attached. One had a booger snuggled up in his right armpit; a second had latched on just above the man's right knee. The other man had a booger hooked on the outside of his right thigh. His head leaned back on the couch, and a booger had latched on over the bottom of the man's chin. The large mouth swallowed the man's lower face from his Adam's apple to the base of his nose.

I realized all the boogers' eyes were open. I could feel their squiggly pupils locked on me as I looked around the room. The reality of the situation was slowly dawning on me.

I was shocked out of my reverie by a gentle touch on my right ankle. I grunted, jerked my leg back and looked down. The booger closest to the doorway had detached. Its body was curled up on the crusty carpet close to my foot, and one slimy arm reached up for me. The booger's jaws spread open, almost like it was yawning. Blood coated the mouth and was caked between the rows of jagged teeth. The mouth closed. The small, reaching claw opened and closed as its eyes stayed locked on mine.

I stepped outside the shed thinking I'd call the sheriff. My cellphone had no service. I walked back to mom's trailer as fast as I could. Using her landline, I dialed the sheriff's direct number. No answer. That was my first clue that something was really wrong.

***

Georgia Screeches

"Mom, I need to move you to bed early tonight. I've got to ride into town."

"Okay. I'm not feeling so good anyway."

***

I was nervous driving towards town. I'd never tried to call the sheriff before, but the fact that no one answered made me anxious. Well, that and seeing six dead bodies with sucking boogers attached.

The streets were empty, but that was typical for a Wednesday night in Kingsboro. There wasn't anywhere for people to go except the Baptist church. The Wednesday night dinner, Bible study and choir practice always drew a crowd.

I headed for the sheriff's office, a squat wood building off Highway 27. There were a few cars in the parking lot when I arrived.

The thing that hit me when I walked in the front door was the emptiness. No one was there. Fluorescent bulbs flooded the room with light. The only sounds were the phones ringing. Multiple phones were ringing over and over. As soon as one string of rings stopped, another started again a second later. Every seat was empty, every desk light was on, but no one was in sight.

I followed a few hallways but didn't see anyone in the offices, break room or restrooms. The final hall led me to the holding cells. One officer was lying face down in the cell area's hallway. A booger rested on the officer's back, and it sucked at the base of his skull. In three cells, people sat on their bunks. Each lifeless prisoner had one booger attached — one on the front of the neck, one on the palm of the hand and one on the sole of a bare foot. All four boogers worked their jaws and watched me as I walked backwards out the door.

***

Driving away from the sheriff's office, I felt real panic.

Thinking of what to do next, I decided to look for more people. My first thought was the Baptist church. Seven minutes later, I pulled up at the old clapboard building. I saw rows of cars, trucks and SUVs. I guessed a huge crowd was inside.

The old door creaked as I stepped into the church's foyer. Nothing but silence greeted me. I walked through a set of swinging doors into the large sanctuary. Jesus and his disciples posed in the stained-glass windows. Men, women and children sat slumped in every church pew. From the entrance, I could only see the back of their heads, but I knew what I was going to find.

As I moved down the sanctuary's middle aisle, I could see each woman and child had one booger. The men generally had two attached. Ankles, legs, hands, necks, cheeks — the boogers had latched on to any areas of exposed skin. Hundreds of booger eyes followed me. There was no movement in the room other than the slight movement of sucking jaws.

I looked to the front of the sanctuary, and a body sat in the preacher's large chair. Brother Jim Reed had grown fat from 15 years of feeding off Kingsboro's dedicated Baptists. Over 6 1/2 feet tall and close to 350 pounds, his large body had three boogers attached. His thick arms hung down beside the chair with a booger hanging from each open palm. A third booger had latched onto his face, its mouth covering his forehead, eyes and nose.

***

Driving home, a plan was forming, but my first worry was for mom. Her weak state left her vulnerable, so I would have to protect her in the best way I could figure. I ran up the steps and rushed through the door scared to find a booger sucking on her shriveled body. She was still in bed, blankets up to her neck. Her face looked calm, and

54

her skin looked smoother than I'd seen it in years.

I pulled back the covers, no boogers. I was scared to touch her, but I checked her pulse. There wasn't a heartbeat. Her chest didn't rise and fall. There was no response when I squeezed her shoulder. She had died peacefully while I was away. I whispered a quick prayer while I held her hand. I covered her up again and kissed her lightly on the forehead.

***

I'm not sure why, but my first thought was fire. Something had gone wrong in Kingsboro, and the only thing I could figure to do was burn it all down.

Mom's neighbor had a crooked old barn, and it held exactly what I needed. I knew I wasn't going to ask for permission, so I drove my car to the property line. I walked toward the leaning building. Inside I found three propane tanks and four red cans of gasoline.

My first stop was the old shack. I was able to drive some of the trail to the creek. I walked the final mile with questions spiraling in my head. The scene was the same. Some boogers had latched to different spots, but the number of boogers and bodies was the same. I walked through the room pouring gasoline on every body and surface.

The boogers watched me, but none of them moved. They only blinked when I poured gasoline on them.

I stepped outside and tossed in a lit match. As the flames erupted, I didn't hear a sound from inside. I watched the door. No boogers tried to escape. Looking inside, I could see the flames crawling over the slimy skin of the closest booger, the one that had reached for me. It stayed attached and showed no reaction or pain.

***

At the sheriff's office, I broke out a window, poured in a can of gasoline and tossed in a lit match. Once the carpet and furniture were burning, I opened a propane tank's valve and chucked it in the window. I heard it pop. After a little while, fire was pouring from every window in the building. I waited for a bit, but I didn't hear any fire trucks coming.

The Baptist church was my next stop. I walked down the sanctuary's middle aisle slinging two cans worth of gas on everybody and booger I could reach. I put an open propane tank on the front altar and one halfway down the aisle. Another lit match and fire raced down the aisle toward the pulpit.

***

I'm back at Mom's now. The sun's up, and I've got a map of town with everywhere else I need to visit circled. I stopped and stole every gas can and propane tank I could find. I still haven't seen a cop car or a fire truck. I don't know what's happening here, but I do know one thing: once these places are burning, I'm going back to Wisconsin.

•

Allan J.D. McNeill is an independent horror author from Edinburgh, Scotland, with no specific connections to Georgia. However, he tends to set his stories in America. "I find it a fascinating country." Allan wrote and self-published a trilogy of stories that ended up becoming his first novel, *Tales by the Campfire*. He followed with, *Diary of a Broken Mind*, *Inflatable*, and his biggest project to date, *Planet of Dinosaurs* which is a novelization of a movie that Allan watched endlessly as a kid. As for Allan's involvement in this anthology, he says, "It is undoubtedly a dream come true and an experience that I will never forget. Horror is life!"

•

Howler by
Allan J.D. McNeill

For centuries, stories—tales have been passed down from one generation to the next. Stories of men with the blood of the beast that can transform from man to beast under the full moon. Blood-thirsty creatures that stalk the lands looking for prey. The lucky ones died at the mercy of such creatures, but the ones that were attacked, but escaped, were not so fortunate, as they would ultimately become 'a howler'. The howler is much larger and more aggressive than their counterparts, but they have one weakness—werewolves transform under every full moon and can sniff out an unchanged howler. Although the howler transforms under a full moon, there is one additional rule—they can only turn if the full moon appears within the final stages of their male child's birth.

Throughout the world, the howlers walk among us. Some know of their curse, but others are oblivious to the fateful change in their DNA, passed down to them from their fathers.

One howler in particular, Robert Travis, husband and father-to-be, a resident of Atlanta, Georgia, was a well-known, highly respected member of the city. Robert knew of his curse but kept it a secret. An architect first, builder second, he single-handedly restored the mansion on the edge of the Fernbank Forest Nature Reserve, that his wife, Kirsten, had inherited when her mother died three years ago. With only two weeks to go until the birth of his first child, Robert had begun to feel strange. Fleeting visions whilst awake, weird tastes in his mouth, the feeling of great strength, and his steaks were getting rarer. It was on the last Friday in October that he began to feel it the most. The thirst for blood was growing ever stronger. As they got ready for bed, Robert's mood changed, and he turned on Kirsten without warning.

Kirsten's red hair fluttered as her mother's antique vase hurtled past her head. The murky water and decaying flowers trickled down the wall in several thin streams. Beneath her flannel nightdress, her heart pounded. Her green eyes were opened wide, unblinking, as she watched her husband reach for the next closest object that he could get his blood-thirsty hands on. His eyes, also open wide, were not human; or at least to her, they seemed otherworldly—almost demonic. He was slowly beginning to change into someone—something that Kirsten didn't recognize anymore. Robert cupped his elongating fingers around the base of the bedside lamp, another of Kirsten's late mother's belongings, and threw it in her direction. She flinched, but the cord saved her. Had the lamp not been plugged in, it would surely have killed her. He growled at her; it was deep and animal-like as he bent down to pick up the solid bronze lamp.

"Robert," she yelled. He looked up and stared at her through eyes as black as the darkest night. He held the lamp in his trembling hands. "Will you please stop this? This isn't like you. Just stop it and we can work out—work out whatever is happening to you together. Robert, please, I know that you're still in there. If you want to kill me, just do it, but please know that I still love you. I always have—always will. Fight it, Robert. Whatever it is—fight it. You're stronger than that beast within you. You can fight it. If you won't do it for me—do it for our baby," she said as she rubbed her belly.

Robert threw the lamp against the wall. It hit with a dull thud, leaving a bowling ball-sized indent in the cracked plaster. Kirsten looked stunned. She could barely lift the lamp, and Robert had just thrown it across the room as if it were nothing more than a paper airplane. He snarled again, but this time, his teeth—my God—his teeth were growing, overlapping his bottom lip. His human teeth fell from his mouth and hit the floor with a hollow rattling sound. "You don't understand, Kir—"

Robert doubled over in pain and clutched his stomach as the transformation continued. His brogues began to split as his feet widened, and his toenails started to pierce the thick leather as they forced their way through. His bones began to snap and contort; his knees snapped backward like a stork. He thrust his head and howled in agony. His father had told him that this night would come, but nothing could have prepared him for the unbearable torture that his bloodline had inflicted on him. The shirt on his back split as the fibers stretched to their limit, exposing an enormous dark-haired back. His spine poked through his skin. "Kirsten! Run! I don't know how much longer I can control the beast. There's a gun in the pantry." He took a deep breath as a sharp pain coursed through his body. He continued as fast as he could whilst he still had some control over his speech. "There's a gun in the pantry behind the hatch above the top shelf. There's a tin box beside it filled with silver bullets. I need you to go and get it, but you'd better hurry. Once the transformation is complete, I won't be me. My morality will cease, and I will hunt you down and kill you. I want you to shoot me in the head. Don't hesitate. Pull that trigger and put me out of this misery. I'll try and give you a head start—a fighting chance. I love you," he said as his voice turned to an ear-piercing howl. With his last ounce of strength, he began to stand on his hind legs. He stood tall, almost nine feet tall.

Kirsten took a step toward him with her hand outstretched. She knew that it was a foolish thing to do, but she wanted to touch him one final time. Her hand trembled uncontrollably. She moved in closer. As her fingertips brushed Robert's mucus-covered snout, he shot out a blast of warm air onto her hand, but before she could stroke the side of his face, the creature took a step back. Its claws clicked on the laminated flooring, and in the blink of an eye, Robert turned and raced toward the closed window and launched himself through it, shattering the double-paned glass. The thud as Robert hit the ground below, a mere thirty feet, was bone-crunching.

Kirsten sauntered cautiously toward the window. A fresh, night breeze blew the curtains, making them flutter in the wind. The hairs on her naked arms stood on end, and she couldn't tell if it was due to the confrontation of the creature, or the sudden change in temperature. She reached the broken window and stared out into the night. The full moon was enormous—low in the sky, so much so, that she felt as though she could reach out and touch its inviting glow. A distant howl chilled her to the core of her body. She focused, adjusting her gaze from the moon, and looked out toward the forest that surrounded their enormous sixteenth-century home. A dark figure, moving away, moving fast, disappeared from view. She placed the heels of her hands onto the window sill, not realizing that splinters of glass were slowly worming their way beneath her skin.

"Robert, will I ever get you back?" she whispered into the darkness, hoping that the breeze would carry her soft voice to him.

Suddenly, the pain hit her hard. She pulled her hand away, and as she tried to remove the glass from her hands, she could hear a series of dull thuds coming from outside. She peered out of the window once again, staring, focusing, her eyes straining to adjust. The sound began to get louder—closer. Then she saw it. The creature was racing toward the mansion, heading straight for the window. It snarled as it came, thick strands of saliva dripping from its jaws. The galloping thuds of its monstrous paws and feet got louder, and the howler got bigger. She so desperately wanted to move—get to the gun, just as Robert had ordered her to, but she was terrified. Her feet felt as though she were glued to the floor. Then there was a knock on the bedroom door, causing Kirsten to turn quick, jerking her neck to the side.

"Hello?" she called out instinctively.

A voice from behind the door whimpered. "Kirsten, is everything alright in there? I thought I heard a window break while I was cleaning the other side of the house. I wanted to come and make sure you're all right. Is Robert okay?"

Why are you still here, Veronica? I thought you'd gone home—"

The thunderous gallops stopped and were followed by a snarl. Kirsten turned just in time to see the howler leap through the air toward the broken window. It caught its arm on a shard of the unbroken window that was still embedded in the frame. The glass tore into its flesh, tearing out a large patch of fur. The howler stood in front of the window, the wind blowing its hair in all directions. It took a step toward her, and with one strike of its arm, it tossed the remaining contents of the dresser on the floor.

"Robert, stop! I know you're still in there some—" The howler slowly stood tall, its head brushing against the ceiling, and took a step toward her. She screamed.

"Kirsten, is everything all right?"

"Veronica, go and hide."

Kirsten, unable to remove her gaze from the howler's eyes, made small steps backward toward the door. She carefully reached her hand out behind her and felt for the knob. She turned it, and when the door clicked, the howler let out a piercing cry then raced toward her. Hastily, she pulled the door open and darted out into the hallway, knocking Veronica to the ground. Kirsten stumbled and almost tumbled over the railing. She only kept her balance by placing her blood-soaked hands on the ivory railing that ran the entire length of the balcony that overlooked the foyer. The pantry was only a short walk, but tonight, she thought that it might as well be on the other side of the world. The howler snarled. Kirsten turned. Veronica, rubbing the back of her head, screamed when she saw the howler squeeze its hulking frame through the doorway.

"Veronica, run!" Kirsten yelled.

Veronica scrambled back, the howler turned its head and focused on her, and for a brief moment, she could have sworn that it had smiled at her.

"Robert," Veronica cried out.

Georgia Screeches

"Robert can't help us, Veronica," Kirsten replied.

"Did this thing kill him?" she asked.

Kirsten shook her head and pursed her dry lips.

"Nope! Veronica—that thing *is* Robert."

The howler lunged toward Veronica and thrust its claw deep into her thigh and sliced down to her ankle, splitting her tights. It leaned in and sniffed at her face. Frozen with terror, Veronica couldn't move. Tears rolled down her face, and from the corner of her bleary eyes, she could see and feel the snout rubbing against her head. Its mouth opened slightly to form a grin, showing off a row of razor-sharp teeth. She closed her eyes and held her breath, hoping that playing dead would make it go away. The howler pulled back and snarled, its saliva filled mouth quivered, then lunged its powerful jaws toward her. Veronica felt enormous pressure as the howlers' jaws engulfed her head and bit down hard. Its teeth dug deep, piercing her eardrums. The sound of skull-cracking filled the air. It bit down harder, and her head began to give way under the immense pressure. Finally, her skull gave up the fight and caved in. Veronica's brain oozed out and filled the howler's jaws. It bit harder, shaking her corpse, and eventually decapitated her.

The howler stood up and turned to look at Kirsten. It opened its mouth, brain, and skull matter dripping from its mouth then tilted its head and swallowed. Kirsten gagged as the lump slid down its throat. The howler began to swallow rapidly as if it were choking. Kirsten took advantage of the moment and raced down the stairs. She hit the foyer floor running and made a beeline for the kitchen. From above her on the balcony, she heard the howler snarl, and she looked up. The howler leapt the railing and landed behind her. She could feel the hot breath on the nape of her neck. It took a swipe at her, narrowly missing the back of her neck. She felt the breeze from the strike. She couldn't stop—she had to get to the gun. With the howler hot on her tail, she reached the door and quickly opened it. As she closed the door behind her, the howler howled as its fingers sliced away from its hand and dropped to the floor. As she stopped briefly for a breath, she glanced down at the digits, and before her very eyes, they transformed from beast to human. The door behind her began to shake and rattle as the howler pounded its fist on the feeble wood. She walked backward, keeping her gaze firmly fixed on the door. The pounding stopped, and she could hear the clicking of the howlers' claws on the floor, becoming more distant. She knew what it was doing. It was going to charge the door and come crashing through. She quickly ran to the pantry, and just as she had envisioned, the howler burst through the door and slammed into the preparation table in the center of the room. Pots and pans rattled around on the hooks above.

"Robert, stop this," she told him in a commanding tone, but the howler took no notice. The howler snarled and ripped the table from the floor and tossed it against the wall to its left. The force and sheer power crushed the refrigerator like a drink can. As the howler moved closer, with every toe clicking step, Kirsten eased her way into the pantry and locked the door behind her. She removed the gun from the box and loaded all of the bullets she could find. She took a deep breath and rubbed her eyes before storming back out of the pantry into the kitchen. She closed her eyes and fired blindly at the howler. It was on the final shot before the rapid clicking of the trigger that the howler let out a screeching sound that chilled her to the bone. She opened her eyes, and on the floor, Robert lay at her feet with a hole in his forehead.

"I'm so sorry—"

Georgia Screeches

Kirsten felt her belly ripple from beneath her nightdress, and as she lifted it up to investigate, a baby howler's claws burst from her stomach before it began to climb out of her slowly. Her screams that rushed into the darkness went unheard.

•

Jonathan Cook is an award-winning playwright and film-maker based in South Carolina. Many of his stage plays have been produced around the world and he's a four-time recipient of the Porter Fleming Library Award. Other notable works include short horror stories that have been featured on the "Chilling Tales for Dark Nights" podcast. More on Jonathan preceding his second tale in this anthology, *The Tear in the Roof.*

•

Becoming
by Jonathan Cook

Ya know, the worst part of all this is the endless chanting. There's a lot of stuff I can take but these monotonous loops of foreign words must stop. I can't even think straight anymore. What is that language they're speaking? I can't make it out. Latin? No. It's gotta be something older. Something...ancient.

"Layirot not'xis, janai it'hit namosh..."

Ahhh...What? Was that me? Why did I just say that? I don't even know what it means. No, it couldn't have been me. It had to be...some sort of a residual echo in my head. Because these robed freaks won't shut up! "Hey! You! Douchey-looking guy with the book! Look at me! Silencio your mouth- o!"

God! They just keep droning on and on! My mind...my ears...all of my senses are growing numb from the sound of their tiresome voices and I can't do a damn thing about it because they've tied me down to...what is this? Some type of stone altar I guess. My wrists…I've rubbed them raw from trying to squeeze them out of this stupid rope. The pain is worth it though. If I can get out of here…away from the dreadful mantra consistently spewing from their lips…the pain is worth it.

They've lit candles along the cavern walls. The dim light makes their shadows dance across the stones and I can see images of strange looking creatures that have been crudely drawn on the rocky surface. Along with some kind of scripture written from one end to the other. I have no idea what any of it says. It's probably the same sort of garbage they've been repeating for the past hour now. "Oh, I just love what you've done with the place. My 5-year-old nephew has similar works of art hanging in his bedroom. You buncha psychos! I'm going to end ALL of you if you don't shut your god damn faces!"

I can't get a reaction from any of them. Not a single one. They won't even look at me. They all just blankly stare across the room toward the markings on the walls. Like a bunch of brainless zombies. Chanting.

There's a rune-ish pattern stitched around the openings of their sleeves and all their robes are white. Except that one there on the ground. He's the first one that grabbed me when Agent Shaw and I arrived. His robe is now soaked in red. I gave that son of a bitch a fair warning. He should've listened.

"…hiyiras fabarent fubet unti…"

Urrrraaaahhhh! Those words…those infectious words…there's a rhythmic cadence in their speech and it's pulsating like a heartbeat in my brain. My mind is warping from the vibrations of their voices. Get out of my head! If they're going to kill me, I wish they would just do it already. They wasted no time slaughtering my partner. What do they want with me? Listening to them speak the same exotic words over and over is utter torture. Just kill me you cowards! Zone everything out. Clear my thoughts. I must. They can't keep going on like this forever.

"...braso da brasol, neesa farath..."

Aahhh...something is happening to me. That lounge singer is to blame. Marie Landau. She's the one who tricked us into coming here. Marie. What a shitty name. I've never in my life known an honest Marie. They're ALL liars and arrogant. I think she knows it too. That's probably why she uses the stage name "Velvet Nightingale" when she performs down at the Pair-a-dice club. I should have known something was up when she came to us. Her story was careless and inconsistent...but she gave us a lead on a missing person case, claiming that she witnessed a young man matching the description near the cave entrance. But it was all just a scam to get us to enter the maze of tunnels within. Deep into this wide chasm for their ritualistic purpose. Marie...she is one of them. I can see her standing alongside all the others in the semi-circle around me. Chanting with them. "You look horrible in white, Marie. I've been meaning to tell you that. Really. Even that favorite white sequined dress you wear on stage makes you look like you have a fake tan."

She's not the only familiar face in the group. There's that lawyer guy Victor Price. His annoying ads are plastered all over town. Can't walk ten feet without seeing this hack's stupid face above the tagline, "Real solutions with the right Price." And there's Ms. Shubert. I can't believe that sweet old lady is a part of this. I wonder if that poodle she carries around so often knows that its owner is a filthy murderer. There's no way of knowing just how long this cult has been active but one thing is for certain, this town has a dark secret. Marie doesn't seem to be the ultimate mastermind behind all of this, though. I'm more inclined to believe she's just a collective tool like the rest of them. But it's obvious that these lunatics carefully planned everything. They used the darkness and their numbers to their advantage when we entered this chamber. Our pistols were swept out from our holsters before we even knew what was happening. We never stood a chance. But they weren't expecting the knife I had tucked away. No, that was a sweet surprise. A surprise they didn't like seeing unleashed on one of their own. It was hard to breathe when they overpowered me and forced my chest into the floor afterwards. Shaw screamed my name as they stabbed him to death only a few feet away from me. I wish there was something I could have done. I wish they would have kill me instead.

"...*cabotes memberote y mas wick...*"

What is happening to me? My eyes are hazing over. The robes...the candles...the primal drawings on the walls...everything is turning into a blur. Their ominous incantation is taking away my sight. How are they doing this with only their words? Oh, my god. Even their voices are beginning to muffle. My thoughts are still with me and I'm conscious but...somehow they've completely shut down all of my senses. I can't move or feel...anything. I don't even know if I'm breathing anymore.

Wait. What was that? I...hear...whispers. Faint whispers bouncing around inside my head. Thoughts that aren't my own...and a cold tingle is spreading across my mind. There's something in here with me! This...this is impossible. Get out of my head! Possession. It must be a form of possession. They've conjured some spirit and allowed it to trespass into my consciousness. It's speaking to me with unintelligible whispers and I can't tune it out. It's all so overwhelming but...oddly there's something calming about it. I'm not afraid but I can't help but tremble at the fact that I should be.

There's a low suppressed rumbling sound beginning to

swell in my ears now. A quiet hum rising in volume. WAIT. I know what that is. The cultists! Their voices are becoming clear again…and…holy shit…I can understand them now. Their language is still foreign, nothing I've ever learned…but somehow…I can decipher the words. Whatever it is they've invited into my mind…this thing sharing my consciousness…it's allowing me to understand them. All of them. Marie. Victor. The other robed strangers. I can interpret them all clearly now.

"…Thou shall descend upon our devout spirits. Embody the ardent soul…"

They've made me…an avatar for some entity they've summoned from another dimension. Their invocation has caused it to materialize inside me.

The candle light…my vision is restoring now as well. But…what is this place? Is this even the same room? The cultists are still here but there is so much more that wasn't here before. Little glowing flecks fill the chamber, hovering in the air. They're all over the room. Fluid sparks floating in and out of existence like I've crossed over into some cosmic plane. And over there…it looks like the beings depicted in the cave drawings have come to life. These otherworldly creatures are positioned across the room from the robed citizens. I can see it all now. It was never a crescent the chanting cultists formed around me. No. These interdimensional beings have always been there. The cult members were merely one half of a grand circle completely surrounding me. My eyes…they just had to be reborn in order to see it all.

My body begins to move but it's no longer under MY control. The ropes binding my wrists that I struggled SO hard to escape from…they easily snap when my hands rise away from the stone. But I am not free. This body is no longer my own. And my mind…my thoughts…they aren't clear anymore. What have I become? Everything is fading.

"I am gone…"

"I am…gone…"

"I…am…Goddess Ardneh. I have come."

•

Another terror tale by Richard Tanner. His Buck Short Productions is pure underground horror coming straight through from Atlanta, with podcasts, interviews and blogs via Facebook at abuckshortproductions, and he created a short film entitled *Hematolangia*, starring Gina Danielle McKay and Ryan Morris.

•

It's Raining Again
by Richard Tanner

The rain poured onto the dark streets of Atlanta. Even at night the streets would still steam up. It was always hot here. Them billows of steam created a never-ending swamp, or so it would seem. It was just that this swamp swarmed with big buildings and urban culture instead of old oak trees and gaters. How much difference is there really between the two though? I tell ya, they both believe in respect, both believe in money and they both love they hometowns. Born and raised in the back woods as opposed to being born and raised in back alleys—that's about all the difference. The kids in the woods, they play with snakes, while them in the city they prefer playing with needles they find. Them country folk they shoot for fun, but then again so do them city folk.

Back before the drought, it had been raining on and off for a solid month, or so it would seem. You know, that was the thing about Georgia then, if you didn't like the weather, ya just had to wait fifteen minutes or so. It would change. Not that many people complained 'cause they was just happy to have a coolness in the air when they sat on they porches or sidewalks. The kids loved it cause they feet wouldn't burn when they walked down the streets to see a friend. The men loved the green grass that grew in they yard. They knew a competition was going on against they neighbors, even though it was always unspoken and the winner never said. The churchgoers, they hear stories told of Noah, while they kids look through windows, praying they won't see someone float by. It was a rainy night in Georgia that night, and the streets still steamed.

At one in the morning no one wants to be on the streets of Atlanta; not the cops, not the homeless, not even the criminals-- they just doing they jobs. It was still faintly raining as one man looked over his shoulder while turning between the tall buildings. It was too dark and too late for anybody to care about this man, as long as he don't care about them. But they was safe, his thoughts and cares were only for the rain. He slowly started talking to himself, just barely audible as he walked.

"It's raining again. It's always raining." He shook the water off his head, only to have more rain take its place. "No matter how far I go, or how long I walk, it never stops. It pours on me. Supposed to make things wash away, them cleansing waters, but never for me." He was starting to sound a bit crazy, his emotions getting the best of him. "The rain only makes all this pain and suffering dig deeper into my skin, makin' it hide its face from the water and take shelter in my very soul. Seems like the only thing rain can do is hide my tears." And, oh, that man was right. That rain came down so hard that it was almost impossible to see his face at all, let alone tears.

"Nobody can see me cry. It's not my place in the world to show my agony. I'm supposed to be strong! Ain't nothin' can harm me!" He was screaming now,

73

thrashing his fist about like a preacher speaking of Hell, but he never took his hands out of his pockets. "What am I without this though; another face in the crowd of wounded travelers begging for a way out? The man stopped talking, hung his head low and walked. He walked down a road he had never seen. A final whisper escaped him, a single bubble in the swamp of a city. "It's always raining."

As that one man walked through the alleys between the tall buildings, ranting to no one and everyone, the rain picked up. When the weather changed, it didn't always change for the better. There was a gunshot that night on the rainy streets of Atlanta and yet the streets still steamed.

•

Singer, songwriter, writer, actor, director, and now published author, Chuck W. Chapman is from Greenville, South Carolina. He's toured the U.S. in various rock bands and recently wrote, directed and starred in the Indie horror film *He Drives at Night*, with Butch Patrick of "Eddie Munster" fame. Chuck has also been a background actor in major motion pictures. Always fascinated by the darker side of human nature, ever since being scared out of his wits by the TV movie, *Helter Skelter* (at a much too early age), Chuck feels that, *"Using horror as a creative outlet is a much more productive way to channel fear and frustration than serial killing."*

•

The Buzz
by Chuck W. Chapman

CHAPTER 1

I just wanted to get some sleep. Was that too much to ask? I had been on the road for what seemed like days and could barely hold my eyes open. Just a few hours of shut-eye and I would be good as new.

I should have stopped an hour ago when I came off the Interstate but thought I could push it another 30 minutes. Now, it had been over an hour and I hadn't even seen another hotel or even a wide spot in the road that I could pull off at. I had never been to White Oak, South Carolina before and now I knew why. There was no reason for anyone to be. A stop light 12 miles ago was the only sign of civilization I had seen since the exit.

Just when I thought I was going to be stuck on the 2 lane for another 45 minutes, I saw a small, single story motel with that precious neon sign with the word "Vacancy" beckoning to me like an oasis in the Sahara. The 6-room hotel had one spot open so I pulled in. Grabbing my duffel from the back seat, I made my way to the tiny office in the middle.

The desk clerk looked about 19 but could have been 16 or 40. He had dark, mussed hair and looked like I'd woke him up.

"One room, one night," I said as he slid the little mouse hole in the window open.

"Thirty-six bucks," he mumbled.

I handed him cash and he slid me the room key. "Number 6."

"Thanks," I said and walked the 40 feet it took me to reach the room. I flipped on the light and looked around. A double bed in the middle of a sparsely decorated room with faded wallpaper that was peeling in spots, but overall, it looked clean enough, and other than a faint musty smell, which quickly dissipated when I flipped on the A/C, I didn't see anything wrong with it. At this point, it really didn't matter. I was spent and could probably have slept on the sidewalk.

I tossed my bag on the chair beside the bed and rummaged thru it for my toothbrush and sleep pants. After a quick restroom trip where I took care of the essentials, I stretched out on the bed. It was surprisingly comfortable and the soft hum of the air conditioning unit was just right for a perfect night's rest.

As I quickly drifted toward sleep however, it started. Just a little at first, but just enough to rouse me from reverie.

Georgia Screeches

Buzzzzzzzz. [Pause] Buzzzzzzzz.

I tried to ignore it, but the more I tried to focus on the A/C's hum, the more pronounced it became: Buzzzzzzzz. [Quiet] Buzzzzzzzz.

I began counting the seconds. Buzzzzzz. "One, two," Buzzzzzzz.

I put the pillow over my head.

Buzzzzzz. [1, 2] Buzzzzz [1, 2, 3] Buzzzz. [1, 2] Buzzzzzz:

I looked around the room. What the hell was making that noise? I saw a red light flashing on and off from inside my bag. Buzzzzzz [1, 2] Buzzzz. It seemed to be in perfect time. I flipped on the lamp and went to my bag. Sure enough, my laptop had been left on. I powered it off and sat back down on the bed. Silence.

I smiled to myself, threw my legs back under the covers and turned off the lamp. Just as I began to feel myself drifting off, I heard it again. Oh so faint, but there, nonetheless. Buzzzzzzz [1, 2] Buzzzzzzzz.

Dammit! I threw back the covers and went back to my bag. The laptop was off but it still seemed to be making that infernal noise. I took it into the bathroom and put it on the sink top and closing the door, stood and listened for a minute. Silence.

I made my way back to the bed and sat down. I could feel the heat rising in my head from the lack of sleep and building frustration. I listened intently for a few more minutes and heard nothing. I shut the lamp back off, slid back under the covers and settled in. I stared into the darkness for long minutes and slowly began to slide slowly into unconsciousness until… Bzzzzzzzzz! [1, 2] Buzzzzzzzz!

Holy crap! I stormed into the bathroom, picked up the laptop and slammed it into the bathtub, shattering it into pieces. I might regret it in the morning, but as of now,

77

I didn't care, just please shut the hell up!

I washed my face and looked at my haggard reflection and red, bloodshot eyes. I needed a new laptop anyway. As I slipped under the covers, I felt a peaceful satisfaction. Gratefully, sleep finally came and as I began to dream, Buzzzzzzzz [1, 2] Buzzzzzzz.

My eyes flew open and as I became oriented with where I was, I looked over to the small digital clock on the worn bedside table and saw the numbers 3:15 AM flashing in time with the alarm. Buzzzzzzzz [1, 2] Buzzzzzzz.

Twelve minutes. I had been asleep twelve whole minutes and some asshole had set the alarm clock for 3:15 in the morning!

I slammed my hand down on the alarm. The display went blank, but the buzzing kept going. I pulled the cord out of the wall and threw it across the room. The buzzing kept going. I threw the covers off the bed and went rampaging around the room like a wildman, unplugging the TV, the air conditioning unit and even smashing my cell phone against the wall. I was laughing maniacally as I dove back on the bed, not even bothering to turn the light off.

I curled into a fetal position and put a pillow over my head, then another. Buzzzzz, [1, 2] Buzzzzzz [1, 2, 3] BUZZZZZ, BUZZZZZZZ. [1, 2] BUZZZZZZZ, BUZZZZZZZ. [1, 2, 3] BUZZZZZZZ. BUZZZZZZZ!!!!!

I couldn't take it. As the tears ran down my face, I slowly began to laugh to myself. I pulled my revolver from the side pouch of my nag and sat back on the bed. Buzzzzzzzz [1, 2] Buzzzzzzz.

Laughing softly, I put the barrel to my temple and pulled the trigger. I saw red, then black, then I saw nothing, and most wonderfully, I heard nothing.

CHAPTER 2

While driving through the backwoods of South Carolina, I found myself in some place called White Oak. I had never heard of it and Siri didn't even have a listing for it. After another 20 miles of nothing, I suddenly realized that I was absolutely exhausted. I saw a small motel on the side of the road. According to the GPS, it would be an hour before I saw another. I pulled into the lone parking spot and went to the office in the middle of the building.

"I need a room for the night."

The sleepy-looking clerk looked at me and said, "Sorry, we're full."

"But the vacancy sign is on and there was no one parked at that room on the end," I said.

"We don't rent that one anymore. Some guy killed himself in there a couple months ago."

"You've cleaned it since then, haven't you?" I inquired.

"Well…yeah," he shrugged.

"Then I'll take it. I'm not afraid of ghosts."

"$36 bucks." He reluctantly slid the key to me.

As I opened the door, I took in the small room. Looked like a normal, cheap motel room to me. I brushed my teeth and got ready for bed. Man, was I beat! I was going to sleep like a baby.

Buzzzzzzzzzz! Buzzzzzzzzzzzzz!

●

Amanda Blanton was born and raised in Stockbridge, Georgia, south of Atlanta, where she lives with her family and pets. Her love of horror shares space with her love of the Atlanta Braves. She considers herself a True Crime junkie, which has only deepened her love for horror. This is Amanda's first venture into writing horror, and her debut as a published writer. Amanda says, *"I've always loved to write but never thought I would be taken seriously. I put a lot of effort into this story and to have been selected has been an absolute honor and privilege."*

●

The Silver Dollar Killer
by Amanda Blanton

The school year was coming to a close and all Jason could think about was his computer final in Mr. Burk's class. Freshman year at Georgia Tech was harder than he thought and he was just looking forward to spending the summer on Lake Lanier with his friends. He was halfway back to his dorm when he started to get an uneasy feeling, like someone was watching him. He shook it off and continued his walk. With each step he could feel his stomach getting closer to his throat, his heart began racing faster as he gathered the nerve to turn around and look behind him.

Flashback to 6 weeks ago. Atlanta, Georgia; April

80

Georgia Screeches

1978. The summer heat was setting in early this year and the city was making national headlines. A madman was terrorizing the city and leaving dead bodies in his path. The police had dubbed him "the Silver Dollar Killer," as he would leave silver dollars in the palms of his victims. So far there were 5 victims and the police had no leads, no suspects, and no idea of where he might turn up next. There were no motives for these killings. This guy didn't give a shit. He was meticulous, skilled, and always two steps ahead. He baffled the police and the FBI as his attacks were random and everyone was a target. The crime scenes were gruesome and terrifying; the murders were overkill, everything in excess and a different means of death each time. Some victims were beaten to death, some strangled, others were shot or stabbed. Basically, whatever mood this monster was in decided how his victims would perish.

The police looked like failures to the whole city, because no one was brought to justice. The APD worked tirelessly day after day, night after night. Every lead they thought they had fizzled and every person they questioned just became another useless name on a piece of paper. Every time anyone went outside, they constantly looked over their shoulder in fear, the mayor issued a city-wide curfew, but after a couple of weeks it didn't matter. The killer lurked in the shadows like a panther stalking his prey, waiting for the right moment to pounce. No one got a look at him until it was too late. The only victim, barely hanging on to life when the police arrived, gave the only clue they had to go on. "He had piercing green eyes." Police were hoping to get more, but in the end, like the others before her, she met her untimely demise. Authorities were hitting brick walls and the body count kept rising.

Jason slowly looked back over his left shoulder,

nothing, he looked over his right shoulder and again nothing. He let out a small sigh of relief as he turned back toward his route. His breathing slowly returned to normal as he realized he'd gotten all worked up for nothing. He took a few more steps and stopped. Standing in front of him was a man about 6' 3" wearing all black, leather gloves, and a face shield. The only part of the man's face that Jason could see were his piercing green eyes. Jason froze. Inside he was screaming, "Get the fuck out of there! What are you doing?!" but outside he just stood there. Frozen. Jason stared down the Silver Dollar Killer and all he felt was emptiness, there was no one behind those eyes. Just darkness. Then everything went black.

Jason slowly regained consciousness. He heard cars driving overhead. He tried to scream but couldn't. He tried to move but couldn't. He blinked a few times to focus his vision and then it connected. He felt wet and cold, but how? It had to be at least 90 degrees outside. He slowly lifted his head and looked down at his body. His blood-soaked body. He couldn't tell how many times he had been stabbed but he knew his time was running out. He didn't have the strength to get up and run but he had enough willpower to turn over. His eyes focused on a pair of black motorcycle boots, almost brand new and neatly tied. He wasn't alone. At this moment Jason knew that this was it, he wasn't going to make it. He thought of all the things he'd done in life, his family, his friends. The Silver Dollar Killer stood over him, grabbed his hair and pulled his head back. Jason felt the blood-soaked blade of the knife meet the side of his throat, he let one last whimper as he felt the blade slice through his skin from one side to the other. And with that it went dark, one last time.

It took police 2 weeks to find Jason's body. He was found in a ravine close to I-75, his throat sliced from ear to ear so deeply that he was nearly decapitated. He had multiple stab wounds on his back, stomach, arms and legs and held a shiny silver dollar in his right hand. Decomposition had been brutal; the Georgia heat hadn't been their friend and multiple officers vomited at the crime scene just off the smell alone. Had it not been for Jason's wallet still being in his jeans it would've taken longer to ID his body.

Three months into the killings, and with no new information or leads, the killer turned it up a notch. The chief of police received a package in the mail, no return address on the outside, no note or message on the inside, just a shiny silver dollar. It was immediately sent to forensics for fingerprinting and testing but came up clean. No prints. No DNA. Nothing. They even tried to trace the package back through the postal system but ultimately came up empty. The police chief received a total of 4 silver dollars and each time lab results and tracking yielded nothing.

The killer disappeared as quickly as he appeared. The time between murders would stretch longer and longer. The police were able to devote more time to trying to solve the murders rather than adding another case to the file. A week went by, then 2, then a month, then 2 months. As New Year's Eve came and citizens rang in 1979, they finally felt like they were able to breathe and sleep peacefully at night. Although Atlanta's time in the national spotlight had come to an end, people were still living the nightmare at home. There were so many unanswered questions and loose ends.

Eventually the anniversary of the first murder came around and police were no closer to finding the person responsible for the heinous crimes. They were still hitting dead ends no matter what the tried. It had been months since anyone was brought in for questioning and to the world every case appeared to have gone cold. Families of the victims still had no closure and were just as angry as they were a year before. The city decided to hold a vigil at Piedmont Park to memorialize the victims and to raise money for their families. Vendors came out and set up to sell food, drinks, crafts, and other items. Everyone was there, including the mayor and various news outlets to cover the vigil and pay their respects.

Jason's family came out for support and were helping run one of the concession booths when a man in his mid-thirties approached. He was wearing a ball cap, jeans and a black T-shirt.

Hi, what can I get for you?" Jason's mom asked politely.

"Just a soda please," the man replied.

"Here you go, that'll be 50 cents," she said as she handed over the bottle.

She smiled as the man met eyes with her, he had the most piercing green eyes. The man smiled back and handed over a shiny silver dollar. Jason's mom looked down at the coin and felt cold chills run all throughout her body. She looked up quickly but the man had disappeared into the crowd.

She tried to scream for help, but no sound escaped her mouth. This was him! The man who took her child from her. She knew it! Her adrenaline started pumping as she ran around the booth and out into the crowd. She looked to the left. She looked to the right. Nothing. She felt defeated. She stopped to catch her breath when out of the corner of her eye she spotted a man in a black T-shirt and ball cap. She took off running, bulldozing through the attendees, when she finally caught up to him. Jason's mom grabbed his arm and quickly spun him around. She immediately stopped.

84

Georgia Screeches

"Can I help you?" the man softly asked.

"Um, ah, no. I'm sorry. I-I thought you were someone else," she stammered back while trying to sound apologetic at the same time.

Jason's mom turned away, took a deep breath, fell to her knees and began crying into her hands.

•

Mike Lyddon is a writer, producer, director and FX makeup artist known for films like *Cut Up, Zombie! vs. Mardi Gras, Horror Anthology Movie Vol. 1* and Vol. 2, *First Man on Mars* and more. Mike filmed over 100 live indigenous and traditional music videos in South America. Having moved to Georgia from Peru a month earlier, Mike stumbled onto a strange house while walking around town. *"I began thinking about why it was the way it was (no windows, one door). I thought it would make for a great horror tale. Right after that, I saw a notice for this Days of the Dead horror anthology!"* The rest is history.

•

The House on Greenville Street
by Mike Lyddon

Even though Edward owned a car, he often preferred to take the long walk into town. The rolling hills of Lafayette County south of Atlanta provided a scenic path that allowed him to observe everything in keen detail, something that driving never affords anyone. And he never took the same route. In this old town constructed in the late 18th century, there were so many ancient curiosities to be found on nearly every street that the idea of taking the same route was just plain boring. After his wife died, he moved from Atlanta and rented a small house here. Edward kept to himself most of the time and he found that taking long walks eased the pain of his loss and kept him from diving into a deep state of depression.

Throughout the two hundred plus years of its existence, the town had seen so many changes it was like a patchwork of history before his eyes. A mansion built in 1880 sat next to an apartment complex from the 1960s. Forgotten train tracks abruptly ended where a weather-beaten strip mall now stood. Towering monuments to an industrial era devoured by Kudzu vines. Beautiful architectural wonders eroding, imploding, and crumbling into the red Georgia clay.

Then there was the local cemetery sprawled on a huge hill southeast of the town center. Edward loved cemeteries. His favorite thing was to find the oldest grave by birth, and this particular cemetery had some fairly old plots. Spanning what must have been twenty acres, it took Edward several trips to cover the entire field. Dozens of huge mausoleums loomed amongst the gravestones, enough to get you turned around and lost if you weren't paying attention. One day, Edward found a small stone marker hidden between some larger plots, perhaps the oldest in the cemetery. "Evangeline Carter - born, 1798 - died, 1835." And carved in the granite below, "I'll see you soon, my love." Only 37 years old. Probably taken by Consumption, Yellow Fever, or God knows what. It was then that he noticed something very peculiar about the surrounding gravestones, markers, and mausoleums. All of the death years were the same. 1835. While it wasn't unusual for a cemetery to have sections of graves from the same era, he thought it was pretty odd that all of these people died in the same year. Continuing on the path, Edward heard a voice in the distance, as though someone was speaking to another person. As he walked around a particularly large mausoleum, he saw an old black man tending to one of the graves. In all of the times he'd visited this cemetery, he'd never seen another person. Edward cautiously approached the man. He didn't want to bother him, but he was interested to see what he was doing. The old man must have sensed Edward was there because he stopped talking to himself in mid-sentence. "Good morning," Edward said.

The old man tilted his head up for a second. "Morning," he grunted and continued pulling weeds from the base of a large headstone.

"I couldn't help but notice that many people in this part of the cemetery died in the same year. Kind of strange, isn't it?"

"The Plague," the old man said.

As Edward walked by him, the man turned around.

"Best not be coming around here at night. There's lights in those mausoleums at night and them back streets ain't safe neither. Best just to stay away."

"Okay, thanks," Edward replied and continued on his way.

Lights? Plague? He wanted to go back and ask, but then he thought the guy was just bullshitting him. Probably doesn't like people wandering around the place, and Edward couldn't really blame him. There were enough stories of idiots partying in cemeteries at night and ripping off gravestones and statues. He was sure the old man had seen his fill.

Edward made it to the northwest edge of the cemetery and was about to turn onto the main road going into town when he noticed something he hadn't seen before. On the left end of the road there appeared to be another, smaller road. As he drew nearer, he saw the old sign which read "Greenville Street" bent at an angle and pulled down by Kudzu vines until it was almost entirely obscured from view. The road itself was crumbling and full of potholes, and a rusted yellow "Dead End" sign dangled precariously from an oxidized metal pole.

"Stay off the back streets," he laughed as he started down the road. The houses were few and far between, and the ones left standing were at least 100 years old or older and most appeared to be abandoned. There was a large blue Victorian house which was certainly gorgeous back in the day, now boarded up with a collapsing roof and the word "DEMO" spray painted in day-glo orange on the door. It seemed like there were more empty lots than houses on the street, the kind of lots with stunning brick and concrete stairs and walkways that once lead to majestic homes, now lead to empty, overgrown spaces reclaimed by nature.

It was then that Edward saw something which made him stop dead in his tracks. Another late 19th-century structure, a white house with a steep A-frame roof at the end of the street. He walked past the house, then walked back again to make sure he wasn't hallucinating or seeing an optical illusion. But it was real, alright.

The house had no doors or windows.

It was solid tongue and groove weatherboard covering the whole thing, and not one opening to be found save for a small wood attic vent near the peak of the roof. *There must be a door in the rear,* Edward figured, but something told him not to go back there to find out. He pulled out his phone, took a few photos and returned to the main street to continue his walk.

That night, Edward lay in his bed wondering why he didn't go behind the house to make sure that there was a door. Obviously, there was a back door. There had to be. Who the hell would build a house they couldn't enter? A web search for the history of Greenville Street turned up nothing, and although it was charted on maps, there was no street view to be found. No historical photos. The more he studied the photos on his phone, the more he knew he had to go back and find out for sure.

The next day, Edward took the same route through the cemetery to Greenville Street. Trespassing be damned! He had to see for himself, even if it meant a run-in with a neighbor or the police. His heart sank as he approached the white house. There was an old 1940s-style Ford delivery truck parked on the left side, backed up so the ass-end was protruding into the backyard.

Screw it, Edward thought as he walked past the truck and to the rear of the house. *Someone is here, and I'll just...*

A chill rolled down his spine as he looked at the back of the house. There was no door, no windows. Edward's mind froze like a robot who is presented with two conflicting truths to the same question. *No doors, no windows...how can this exist?*

This cannot exist, yet it does.

As he stepped backwards to get a better look at the roof, his left foot landed on an uneven surface and he momentarily lost his balance. He looked down and realized he was standing on a door that was framed and set horizontally into the ground.

What the hell? This is the entrance?

Edward carefully opened the door and stared into the blackness below. He could see some steps descending down to what appeared to be a concrete floor. Suddenly he heard the sound of someone whistling in the passage, and it was rapidly getting louder. He carefully closed the door and walked off the property and back down the street. As he headed for home, Edward considered the possibilities. Were they running drugs? Bootleg moonshine? Human trafficking? The truck was big enough to stuff a few dozen people into it. No, no. He was just being paranoid. There's probably some perfectly reasonable explanation. Either way, he was going to find out tonight. He wasn't going to endure another night of wondering what the hell was going on.

At 11pm, Edward entered the old cemetery armed with a flashlight, a lock-pick and a 6-inch blade. He thought twice about bringing his revolver. He could handle the knife well enough. It was a clear, cool night, and the great mausoleums loomed much larger and creepier under the pale moon. As he approached the perimeter road, out of the corner of his eye he saw a flickering orange light. *There was a light moving in one of the mausoleums.* He quickened his pace and reached the road, veering left toward Greenville Street. The dead silence was unnerving, and he knew he'd have to be at least as quiet in order to carry out his plan. Luckily, the old truck was no longer there, so Edward moved in the shadows along the side of the white house until he was in the backyard at the door in the ground. He opened the unlocked door ever so slowly, descended a few steps, and closed it carefully above his head. He turned on the flashlight and began following the passage leading back under the house. It was remarkably clean and well maintained, not the cob-web shrouded, rat infested pit he thought it would be. Soon he reached another short flight of steps, this time leading to a normal, vertical doorway. It was also unlocked. So much for the valuable contraband hidden inside. He felt his right jacked pocket to make sure his hunting knife was still there as he slowly stepped inside. As he scanned the room with his flashlight, a huge grin spread across Edward's face. The room was gorgeous, decked out with 19th and 20th-century antique furniture, huge classical paintings, and a spotless wall-to-wall Berber wool carpet below his feet. And the answer suddenly came to him. This house was owned by some eccentric old family who wanted to keep their possessions a total secret from the world.

But if that was the case...why keep the doors unlocked?

Suddenly Edward heard the rumbling of a large vehicle pulling up to the side of the house. The old Ford truck. He quickly made his way past the main room and hid behind the door of the adjoining smaller room, keeping it cracked open just enough... He listened intently as the truck doors opened and closed, followed by hushed voices and occasional laughter leading to the back door. He heard it creak open followed by the sound of many footsteps descending the short flight of stairs and in turn ascending the stairs to the main room. The voices were clearer now, a mix of males and females talking and laughing as they entered the house. Edward had never pissed himself in fear before, but he was damn close now. He literally had no place to run to, trapped like a rat and at the mercy of these people. It was then that one of them switched the lights on revealing an incredible sight...they were all attired in 19th-century clothes complete with wigs and makeup!

My God, it's some kind of Victorian Cos-play party, Edward thought, *and it's amazing!*

A beautiful girl dressed in a white silk gown wearing a large feathered hat played Liszt's "Mephisto Waltz" on a perfectly maintained Victrola while the others poured glasses of wine and laughed and strutted around the parlor without a care in the world.

I'm a total idiot, Edward realized. *This place is just some kind of secret party house for these peoples' eccentric Victorian soirées.* A warm feeling of relief passed through him as he gazed in admiration at the partiers having the time of their lives.

The hell with it, I'm just going to go out there and introduce myself. Edward slowly opened the door and waved his hands in a "Don't worry, I'm harmless" manner as he entered the room.

"Uh...Hello everyone. I know this seems weird, but please let me explain..."

They all stopped suddenly and turned in unison to stare at Edward.

Oh shit, Edward thought.

Then they all burst out in uproarious laughter and clinked their wine glasses together in approval.

The pretty girl at the victrola smiled. "No need to be concerned, my silly boy, you're absolutely welcome. And absolutely perfect!" They all laughed again. "Welcome to our party house, monsieur. It is but our humble home away from home." Her eyes gazed in the direction of the cemetery. Edward shivered. A young man dressed in dark blue with a long coat and top hat stepped forward.

"Dearest Evangeline, please don't play with your...guests like that." He said tipping his hat in her direction. More laughter from the group.

Evangeline? The name on the grave...

The door opened again and the old black man from the cemetery entered the room. The gentleman in the top hat removed a stack of bills from his long coat and gave them to the man.

"Excellent job as always, Johnny."

Johnny smiled and took the money, then he looked at Edward and sneered, "I told you not to go to the cemetery at night, but you stupid white boys never listen..heh." And with that, he was gone.

Edward could hear the truck pull out of the driveway as the party-goers turned their attention back on him. They all smiled, revealing their long, sharp teeth in the flickering light of the old lamps.

The plague...

As the vampires descended upon Edward and tore into his flesh, sucking the precious life-blood from his body, his last thought looped over and over again in his fading mind.

Never take the same route...Never take the same route...

END

•

Horror lover, screenwriter, and actress, Alison MacInnis is also something few people can claim to be: the Pink Power Ranger "Dana Mitchell" in *Power Rangers Lightspeed Rescue*. Alison's love of the genre has grown up with her, and today, most of her favorite screenplays and stories she writes are horror-related. Alison's relationship to Georgia is primarily through her travels to conventions and other work, but she is a disciple of old American folklore and rural mythologies, as you'll find in her story. Alison is a triple threat: smart, talented, and scary!

•

Glow

by Alison MacInnis

Raucous laughter rings through the sunlight-dappled Appalachian forest as a crew of five incredibly fashionable 20-somethings carry backpacks with rolled sleeping bags and stylish metal water bottles. They trudge along the worn trail, phones in hands, following two local tour guides sporting dirty coveralls and matching trucker's caps emblazoned with bright blue "Al's Worm Tours!" Close ahead is the entrance to a cave.

In the lead, Chaz stops and holds up his phone, checks his hair, then motions to the others. "Tamarind! Alvie! Come here. Ty, Bry…..you two behind them.

Bry and Ty, twin brothers in coordinating pastel skinny-fit overalls, both grimace. "Why do we have to be in back?" Ty whines.

"Pretty sure we were in back last time," Bry adds.

Chaz doesn't turn; he speaks to their images on his screen. "Feel free to join the rednecks up ahead, I'm sure they'd love to get to know you a little more intimately."

Alvie, beautifully androgynous, snickers as he flicks nonexistent dirt from his pristine white hoodie. "The big one was checking out your asses, he's definitely into you."

"Shut up." Ty steps into place, pulling Bry along with him.

Chaz waits a moment while everyone primps. "Okay, here we go. Hey y'all! We made it to the cave!" Chaz flips the view around to show the cave and guides. "As you can see, our fearless guides have shown us the way to the mythical glow worm caverns of Hawkinsville, Georgia! It took days, hiking through wilderness, braving dangers—"

"Hold up, Chaz." Tamarind raises her hand.

Angry, Chaz stops recording. "What the hell?!"

"*Sorry*, but you'll be fact checked by the haters, these caves aren't days from the town, and it's about as dangerous as running to WalMart after midnight." Tamarind shrugs. "Your call, this one's going on your channel."

"Oh my God, as if it matters! And it's called *embellishing*, it's only what Hollywood does in every story ever told! How about you stick to your makeup tutorials, I'm sure your fans would love to hear what products don't

96

melt off your face in this godforsaken humid piece of shit state. Anyone else have any pointless bullshit to add? No? Then let's go again." Once more, Chaz frames the screen. "Hey y'all! Chaz and crew here, we made it to the mythical glow worm caves of Hawkinsville, Georgia! We're going to head inside and set up camp for the night! Ready guys?" The others smile and wave to the camera. "Let's go!"

Chaz swings the camera around and approaches the cave entrance. The waiting guides grimace at the camera as it swings their way. "This is Big Al and Little Joe local worm guides, and, worm hunters, extraordinaire. You heard me right, *worm hunters*. These intrepid souls brave the wilds of Georgia daily to collect worms. Sirs, inquiring minds want to know, are there that many worms that you can really come out here every day and gather them? Also, what does one do with so many worms?"

Ty and Bry cover their snickers. Little Joe stares blandly at the pair until they sober, smiles melting away. "Yes. Fishin'." The man flicks on a huge lantern, as does Al. "We'll lead you in, then turn off our lights so you can see 'em glow."

"Why don't we get lanterns?" Alvie whines. "I hate the dark.

Al shrugs. "Don't need 'em. Cave ain't miles deep, trail is easy to follow. Plus, your eyes'll get used to it."

The guides head into the cave, followed by the others, who quickly turn on their phone flashlights as the darkness swallows the receding daylight. The cave is dry and dusty, with no worms in sight.

97

"I don't see any worms, Chaz, and it's cold in here. Like, really cold," Alvie whines again as he zips up his hoodie and covers his head.

"Too dry at the entrance, have to get in a bit," Little Joe informs them. "Ain't far."

"Far enough without proper flashlights, our phones are going to eat through our portables." Bry pulls a slim charger from his pocket and plugs in.

"You should wait till it needs it…I'm not giving you mine,'" Ty warns.

"Fuck you."

"Fuck *you*!"

The brothers sneer at each other as the party turns a corner, heading into even deeper darkness. The walls now seem to gleam with moisture, and ahead, a faint blue glow emerges from the darkness, growing in brightness as they enter a huge cavern. Ridges across the ceiling are filled with what look like clusters of luminous blue jellyfish, tentacles hanging down, motionless.

Al and Joe lead them into the center of the space. "This here is where you set up camp. We got a few rules you gotta follow, else the county'll fine you."

Chaz moves closer, filming the men who squint at the light. "First, no fires, the smoke can kill the worms. You wanna cook, go outside, there's a fire pit near the Porta Potty. That's number two…"

The twins snicker at the unintended pun, Tamarind elbows them as Big Al blithely continues. "Don't shit in the cave. Don't piss on the walls. We find any trace—"

Georgia Screeches

"Yeah, yeah, fines, we got it." Chaz rolls his eyes and motions with his hand for them to hurry up.

Al narrows his eyes. "Third, don't touch the worms. You can film 'em all you want, but no touchin'. That goes for poking with sticks, throwin' rocks, or anythin' else you might fancy. Don't do it."

Al looks at Joe. "Anythin' else?" Joe shakes his head, no. "Well then, we'll be off."

Tamarind lowers her camera. "You're *leaving*?!"

Al and Joe turn to leave. Chaz blocks their exit. "We paid for a fully guided experience. All you did was bring us here!"

Al shrugs. "We guided you here, we'll guide you back tomorrow, that's "fully" guided. Didn't say nothin' about sleepin' out here."

Alvie looks ready to cry. "Chaz, we came, we saw, let's just leave! This is stupid, why stay the night?!"

Chaz regards Alvie a moment before turning to Al and Joe. "At least leave your flashlights, we'll need them to go to the bathroom tonight."

Al shrugs again and hands his lantern to Chaz. "Keepin' one, light's gonna fade before we make it back to the truck. See you tomorrow."

The crew watches as the guides disappear around the bend. Chaz sets the lantern on the floor and they cluster around its meager glow, removing backpacks and setting up a makeshift camp, filling the cavern with incredible noise as they fill their battery-operated blow-up mattresses. Ty wanders over to a wall and aims his phone at a writhing mass of worms. "Oh Jesus, these things are gross!"

"Gross! Look at them! They're huge!" Tamarind shudders, moving her light across the pale, slimy looking worms.

Chaz is taking a slow 360 shot of himself looking around in awe and disgust. "Make sure you guys get a lot of insert shots of your own reactions, I'm not wasting any space on you."

Ty and Bry are using their lights to search along the ground. Bry grunts as he trips on a rock. "Those assholes must have removed all the sticks from in here, I can't find anything."

Tamarind laughs. "Oh yeah, from the numerous trees lining the cave walls, idiots. Why do you need sticks?"

"Obviously, we want to poke the worms," Ty replies loftily.

"You post that on your own channel, I'm not paying fines for your idiocy." Tamarind rummages through her pack and pulls out packages of food. "Anyone else want to head back to that fire pit?"

Alvie's stomach rumbles. The others laugh and retrieve their food packages. Chaz takes lead with the lantern and heads back the way they came. Bry trips on another rock, frustrated, he picks up the rock and chucks it at the ceiling, turning away before it hits. None of them see the resulting explosion of glow when the small rock embeds into a mass of worms, damaging several soft bodies, severing pieces which fall onto the bedrolls below.

100

Georgia Screeches

The glow slowly fades as does the chatter and laughter of the oblivious influencers.

With the moon and the stars covered by verdant forest, the outside darkness is nearly as unrelieved as in the cave. The lantern is turned off, and the crew huddles around the fire pit munching on gourmet tofu weenies, smacking biting bugs, and snapping selfies. Tamarind smashes a huge mosquito on her arm, leaving behind a smear of blood. "Gotta hand it to you Chaz, this place sucks more than anything else you've found."

"Second that," Alvie nods.

"Third."

"Third." Ty and Bry simultaneously add. The brothers glare at each other.

Chaz sets down his phone, plugging it into a charger. He finishes the last bit of his weenie and wipes his hands on his pants. "Why are you here?"

The others exchange glances with each other. Alvie raises his hand, which makes Chaz disdainfully shake his head. "This isn't second grade, you tool. You are here because you want numbers. *My* numbers, *my* followers, who will follow you because I tell them to, but they won't *keep* following you unless you keep doing things like *this*. Every day there's a shit ton of fucking brain-dead idiots who think the world wants to know who they are. One in a million gets the audience they need to survive, *I* am that one, and *you* guys are the brain-dead idiots trying to feed off my crumbs and build an unwilling audience. So maybe a little less bitching and a lot more thanking me for saving you from being WalMart greeters alongside your

101

grandads." Chaz picks up his phone and begins scanning through footage.

The others stare at Chaz with wide eyes. Tamarind stands and heads to the Porta Potty, quietly latching the door behind her. Ty and Bry share a glance, then stand, not looking at Chaz as they pass, heading to the trees where they search for long sticks. Alvie is biting his nails, looking worried, but finally gathers his meager courage.

"That was harsh, Chaz."

"Truth usually is."

"We're your friends, but you treat us like shit."

Chaz glances up from his phone with a sneer. "Oh really? Where did we meet?"

"InfluencerCon."

"Right. And what was I doing when we met?"

Alvie's eyes narrow, thinking about it. "Signing autographs?"

Chaz nods. "What were you doing?"

Alvie's face falls. "Asking you to sign something."

"And how much has your audience grown since I've allowed you on my channel? How much have *all* your numbers grown?"

Alvie sighs. "Like, a thousand percent."

"Then maybe you all should shut the fuck up unless you're thanking me." Chaz returns his attention to his phone. Alvie bites his nails. Ty and Bry return with two long sticks just as Tamarind walks past and grabs the lantern. Chaz looks up. "Hey, what do you think you're doing?"

Georgia Screeches

"I don't recall anyone saying this was yours. I'm heading back in. This place sucks, this trip sucks, and I for one am completely over the bullshit. When we get back to LA, I'm deleting my accounts. Fuck influencers and fuck *you*." Tam flips Chaz the finger and heads to the cave. Ty, Bry and Alvie stare after her, stunned.

"Bitch," Chaz seethes. At the cave entrance, Tamarind turns on the lantern Ty and Bry hurry after her. "What about you, little shit? Gonna go kiss the cunt you wish you had?"

"You're foul, Chaz. Just stop." Alvie hurries after the others, leaving Chaz staring after.

Tamarind is in her bedroll, softly chatting with Alvie. Bry and Ty are filming each other poke worms, laughing when the glow increases.

"You guys, this is so sick, they don't just glow, they *slime*!" Bry knocks a worm off the wall and steps on it, making it explode with slime.

"Snot worms! Wonder how long it'll glow?" Ty and Bry stare at each other, then grin. They begin using their sticks to gather worms, winding them around the stick. The twins are laughing hysterically, chasing and whacking each other with the dropping slime balls.

Tamarind shakes her head. "You guys are going to get us banned from the entire state."

"No loss there," Alvie sneers. "I hate this place. Get me back to LA and my glorious bug free city of metal and concrete."

Ty, as covered in glowing slime as his brother, holds his worm ball in his hands as Bry films him hefting it up and down, suddenly launching it straight into the air. It splatters on the ceiling in an explosion of worms and slime which rains down onto everyone. Alvie and Tamarind squeal, hysterically pulling worms and slime from their hair and clothing. Ty and Bry laugh like loons and take a series of slimy selfies.

"That was awesome!" Bry high-fives Ty, then turns to a wall, proceeding to urinate on as many worms as he can manage. The upset worms glow even more brightly than those who had been pulled into a ball. "Ooooh, they don't like that!"

Ty laughs and joins him. "Take that, snot worms!"

"Fucking idiots! This stuff is everywhere! I feel it in my shirt! God, I think it's in my pants!" Tamarind is frantically trying to clean herself.

"It's all over the sleeping bags, this is disgusting. If we get in trouble, *you* two are taking the full blame. Those rednecks are going to fine the shit out of you." Alvie is scratching his neck. The scratching intensifies, he's now scratching everywhere. "I think I'm allergic to this shit!"

Tamarind is starting to itch. "Me too, we need to wash this slime off!"

The twins are itching, looking a little worried, they have a lot more slime on their skin, which is starting to turn red. "Water!" Bry dives for his water bottle and douses his face and hair. He pulls off his shirt and Ty screams, pointing at his chest, which has glowing larvae crawling beneath the surface.

Georgia Screeches

"What the fuck is that?!" Ty screams again as he pulls off his own shirt, revealing more glowing larvae.

Tamarind and Alvie watch, horrified, then peel up their shirts. Larvae. They scream and tear at their skin, shedding clothing, their skin is alive with movement. Ty and Bry are riddled with larvae, every inch of skin is writhing and glowing, they fall to their knees, skin splitting, screams cutting off as tiny glowing worms pour from their ruined bodies, not even leaving skeletons behind. Tamarind and Alvie are in no better shape, they scream piteously as their bodies dissolve into worms.

The cave is silent, filled with unearthly blue glow. Chaz quietly steps from the shadows, eyes wide, filming. After a moment more, he grins, turns on the flashlight, and leaves. In the darkness, his final words echo...

"Fucking genius."

•

Jonathan Cook is a Georgia based actor, director. He's written award-winning plays produced internationally and was a semi-finalist in the 37th annual Samuel French Off Broadway Festival in New York with his post-apocalyptic play, Lobster Man. He's a four-time recipient of the Porter Fleming Literary Award. Aside from playwriting, Jonathan's a filmmaker. His latest film, *Don't You Dare*, is a dark supernatural drama recently screened at the Poison Peach Film Festival in Augusta, GA. Jonathan says his greatest fear is, *"The possibility of outliving all my closest friends and family."*

•

The Tear in the Roof
by Jonathan Cook

The I cannot tell you for certain what it is or how it knows my name but I swear to you that thing is not my husband. The truth will likely make you think I've gone mad or that I'm unhinged from reality…but I *must* tell you about that night – that night we discovered a tear in the roof.

It was our anniversary. We had plans to go out that evening, but there was a harsh storm looming and we didn't want to risk being stranded if Sweetwater Creek was to flood the roads again. So, Richard suggested that we make a romantic night of it at home instead. Music. Candles. Just like when we were younger, he said. His

106

magnetic charm was still as fresh as the day we met and he could tell just by the look on my face that I was all in on this idea.

Half-melted rosemary-scented candles were lit and the jazz tune "Sophisticated Lady" spun on the record player as we danced in the foyer. Richard joked that Ellington wrote that song with me in mind. I would've given him a better smile if I had known that would be the last time I'd ever receive one of his compliments.

Suddenly, we heard a loud ripping sound from above and tiny bits of the ceiling drifted down on us. The southern autumn wind was heavy that night, so we thought maybe a tree had fallen onto the house...but there were no branches in sight. The tear was clean and precise like something razor sharp had scratched through the roof. A gust of cool air whistled as it passed through it. The lights flickered and then blacked out completely...and the sound of the jazz piano faded.

There was a slow but steady flapping sound like wings coming from outside. Richard shined a flashlight through the ceiling...and I swear to you...something was gazing right back at us.

He told me to go to the garage and grab a tarp big enough to patch up the ceiling. So, I ran as fast as I could, and I searched in darkness until I felt the bundled vinyl at my fingertips. A deafening crash then erupted from the front room and it startled me, but it was nothing compared to Richard's scream that followed. His terrified voice sent chills to every nerve in my body. I left the tarp and grabbed the pistol from the lockbox instead.

When I peeked around the corner, I noticed the tear in the roof was now an enormous hole. The beam from the flashlight wavered as Richard shook with fright...and standing before him...was the silhouette of something unimaginable - a towering thing with wings...and what appeared to be tusks. It fiercely grabbed his neck and tore through his shirt revealing his bare chest…and with its talons…it began slowly carving symbols into Richard's skin.

He gasped for me to run as the creature's fingers tightened on his throat…but I froze. Speechless. Helpless. My body refused to move. The marks that thing had carved into the chest of my beloved…it looked like some archaic language…maybe runes of some kind. It then…sliced open his stomach causing some of his insides to pour out - oh god, it was such a terrible sight. And that's when Richard stopped fighting back. No more struggle. No movement. His lifeless arms hung there at his sides. And then I saw the creature shove its clawed hand inside him…like he was a puppet or something.

I aimed the pistol – shaking, unable to breathe. The gunshot rang in my ears, but it was nowhere near as loud as the resounding screech that thing made as it turned towards me - a screech of anger, not pain. The ghastly beast spread its massive wings and took on a primal aggressive stance - thrusting it's pointed jaw, looking down on me like helpless prey. There was matted mane-like fur along its neck and shoulders and wet reptilian skin everywhere else, shining in the dim light coming from the window. Tiny horns along its forehead cast shadows across its scaly face. I grew cold watching it move with calculated steps and cat-like focus. The downpour picked up outside and a deep thunder rumbled. A pungent smell of dirt hung in the air like a freshly dug grave. My heart pounded as the creature slowly circled around, it's unforgiving eyes locked on me. A sense of dread poured over me like I was gazing into the pits of hell. I shouldn't have hesitated…but those eyes…they haunt me to this day. Before I could fire another shot, it took my arm clean off with its talons.

I can't remember any pain…but seeing the blood pouring out of where my arm once was…that was the moment I fainted on the floor across the room from my dead husband.

I awoke in a hospital bed - fresh bandages wrapped around my arm. The lightheadedness lingered for a while but when I came to my senses I cried to the nurse. "That thing killed my husband" I told her repeatedly when she entered the room. But she kept insisting that everything was alright.

And then…I heard a familiar voice…and I saw that familiar face. It looked like Richard standing before me…but I knew it wasn't. It was the eyes that gave it away – those same haunting eyes I saw in the foyer. And when it leaned down to kiss my forehead, that confirmed it even further. The loose-fitting shirt hung just low enough for me to catch a glimpse of one of those markings etched on its chest.

Perhaps it's some form of black magic…or maybe that creature planted something inside Richard that reanimated his shell of a body – whatever the method, it's only a trick to make you think it's human. I have no clue what it is but I promise you that it has a sinister purpose.

I know what he's told you. That our roof caved in from the high winds. That my arm got severed from the debris that fell. But none of that is true. You've gotta believe me. Ask him to show you his chest. Ask him what song we danced to that night. There *is* proof…if you are willing to find it.

•

Anthony Taylor is a screenwriter, author, and journalist whose works include *Arctic Adventure!*, an official *Thunderbirds* novel based on the British TV series as well as *Voyage to the Bottom of the Sea: The Complete Series - Volume 2*, and much more. Anthony's articles have appeared in *Famous Monsters of Filmland, Fangoria, Screem, FilmFax* and most genre magazines. The many classic elements in his story, *Topstone*, are like a bloody sharpie plotting a course across the map of horrors past toward future terrors.

•

Topstone
by Anthony Taylor

"Get up, you little fairy."

Survival was the better part of valor so Davy remained curled in a ball on the sidewalk. Eventually Tony would lose interest in him and move on to search for another victim.

A gob of spit landed on the sidewalk next to his face.

"Yeah, that's about what I figured, you little monster-loving queer." The bully skulked off.

Davy stayed down, watching him walk away. Lifting his head, he uncurled his body and dusted himself off. His ribs and butt throbbed from the blows he'd received, but he wouldn't even be bruised tomorrow. The misery of being a fourteen-year-old seemed to never stop, but he'd gotten used to it.

A shadow fell over him. He tensed.

Georgia Screeches

"You should stand up to him. My dad says that's the only way to get rid of a bully." Eric lowered his hand, pulling Davy up. The two boys were a study in contrast; Davy's big ears made his face look even leaner than it was, framing sharp cheekbones over sallow cheeks. Eric's crew-cut and thick, horn-rimmed glasses made his face look broader and chubbier somehow. Both of them had taken a few blows from Tony DeMarco, but today had been Davy's turn.

"Bigger fish to fry, pal. But I'm making plans for him, just you wait and see... he'll get his." Davy reached down to pick up the copy of Famous Monsters of Filmland magazine that had fallen out of his pocket. The cover illustration of Lon Chaney peered maniacally at him as he refolded it and put it back. The boys walked down Framingham to Mulberry, and turned at the Western Auto store towards their neighborhood.

"Hey, you wanna stop at Woolworth's and look at comics?" Eric asked.

Davy considered it for a moment. Eric loved Superman, even carried a Superman lunchbox to school every day. Davy preferred the kind of comics they no longer printed; the lurid horror stories published by E. C. Comics in titles like *Vault of Horror* and *Tales from the Crypt*. He sometimes found dog-eared copies at rummage sales or in thrift shops, and always considered such finds a victory.

"Nah, I gotta get home and work on stuff for Halloween. Only a month away, you know!"

Eric looked disappointed. "Ok, I'll go it alone then. Up, Up, and Away!"

***

At home, Davy took his monster magazine and put it atop the stack on the desk in his bedroom. He noticed one of the pages had ripped and was sticking out like a flap of

111

torn skin. *"TONE"* it said at the bottom corner of the page. Grabbing a roll of tape, he opened the book to repair the damage.

"TOPSTONE" screamed the full word across the bottom of the advertisement, followed by *"MASKS!"* It was an ad he'd seen in earlier issues. Famous Monsters handled fulfillment for all the items advertised in their magazine through their mail order arm, The Captain Company. Reading page after page of ads for monster toys, books, films, records, and other gee-gaws was as much fun as reading the articles.

"RUBBER MONSTER MASKS! Moving Face Monster Masks are here at last! Wear one of these and every time you grin or growl, the mask does the same thing! Especially created for us of heavy latex rubber. Fit loosely on the face for extra comfort and go over the top of the head. All masks hand finished and hand painted. Drive girls crazy! Make everyone shudder in fright!"

Davy seriously doubted the masks would drive any girls crazy who weren't already there to begin with. The drawings of the masks showed Frankenstein, a werewolf, a gorilla monster, something called a "Shock Monster" that resembled Mr. Hyde, and a handful of others, all for the low price of $2.25 each. Between the male vampire and ghoul masks, Davy saw a mask he'd never seen before... The Bully. Amazingly, it even looked a bit like Tony DeMarco, with exaggerated, bulging eyes, and giant sharp teeth.

"That's new." He read the copy below the illustration. *"THE BULLY. Give this mask to your worst enemy, then watch what happens!"* What could possibly happen? Maybe it would contract and strangle your enemy. Maybe it was filled with acid and would horribly disfigure them. What if it made them see every bad thing they'd ever done to someone through the eyes of their victims? *What if it revealed their true face to the world so that everyone could see the kind of monster they were inside?*

Davy smiled, that was the best. He opened the desk drawer and took out a Hav-A-Tampa cigar box. Davy opened it and counted $2.25 from the coins inside.

***

"Man, I guess you got a little more banged up yesterday than I thought." Eric was waiting for him at the corner to walk to school. Davy gingerly rubbed the scrape on his chin.

"Yeah, guess so. How was Woolworth's?"

Eric held up a comic. "Got the new Jimmy Olsen! They had Lois Lane too, but I don't buy that book." The boys walked together, occasionally kicking a rock, or stooping to pick up a bottle cap.

"Why don't you buy Lois Lane?"

"Well... she... she's for girls," Eric stammered.

Davy looked at the cover of the Jimmy Olsen book, which showed Jimmy watching an alien girl on television, while fantasizing he was Superman.

"Jimmy Olsen's Super Romance!'? So, tell me how this book isn't for girls?"

Flustered, Eric snapped back at him immediately, "Jimmy Olsen is Superman's PAL. Lois Lane is Superman's GIRLFRIEND. BIG difference."

Davy laughed, "Ok, if you say so, Charles Atlas."

The October wind pushed them along to school.

***

The weeks dragged. On Mondays, Tony DeMarco rolled Davy for his lunch money, and on Fridays he got rolled again for good measure. Leaves fell, dogs got shaggier, and sleeves got longer. Woolworth's provided Eric with new issues of both Action Comics and Superman, and Davy got the new issue of Famous

Monsters with Basil Rathbone on the cover. He noticed that the Bully mask was not in the Topstone ad in the new issue.

Checking the mailbox for the mask became ritual, and finally one day it paid off.

Return address - The Captain Company, P.O. Box 430, Murray Hill Station, New York, NY, 10016. Davy hefted the large, padded envelope and felt of it thoroughly. For a moment he panicked; what if it was just another mail order rip-off like the X-Ray Specs (paper "lenses" with a feather between them), or the Giant Life Sized Frankenstein Monster (flat printed cardboard with metal brads for joints), or the Remote-Controlled Ghost (a balloon, a white plastic sheet, and some fishing line) that he'd ordered? What if it did absolutely nothing to his worst enemy but piss him off further?

Davy walked off the path to avoid the hornet's nest on the side of the garage, that his stepfather had been after him to remove for a month, and went inside. Surely there were truth in advertising laws regulating the making of wild claims in monster magazines sold to kids? Safely in his room, Davy opened the envelope and laid eyes on his prize. No mail order rip-off, this.

This was a thing of evil beauty.

"Boy, do I have plans for you."

***

Finally, the night came; Halloween was on a Wednesday. Everyone scurried home from school to don masks, sheets, makeup, and costumes for trick-or-treating. Jack-o-lanterns were lit, candy was emptied into bowls for kids to pick through, and grownups poured themselves a drink, settling in to wait for the endless knocks and doorbell rings to come.

Davy spent the afternoon preparing for his greatest

Georgia Screeches

trick ever, the glorious result of which lay behind him on his bed, sealed in a medium sized box tied shut by a length of twine. Dressed as Dracula with cape, jacket, and Transylvanian medal on a ribbon, he stood before his mirror, applying white greasepaint to his face and looking at the box nervously over his shoulder in the mirror. He winced as the white makeup covered a bruise on his cheek received that afternoon. A short knock on his door, then it opened.

"Hey Sport, just a reminder. Your mother and I are going to the McDevitt's party at 8:00, you'll need to be back by 7:45 so we won't be late. Capisce?" His stepfather gave him a glare and made a "thumbs up" sign.

"Ok."

"Sorry about earlier. You know you should have gotten that hornet's nest down a long time ago. Right?"

"Right."

"Ok, then." The door shut. Davy rubbed black greasepaint around his eyes.

***

Just after sunset, Davy hit the streets carrying his box and a grocery bag from the IGA for candy, the kind with string handles. Eric met him on the corner dressed in ill-fitting Superman pajamas with a red towel around his neck and a sack of his own.

"I couldn't wear my glasses 'cause then people would know my secret identity. What's in the box?"

"A surprise for Tony DeMarco," Davy said. He looked around as though the bully might jump out from behind a bush at any moment.

"Cool."

Dracula and chubby Superman made their way door to door, knocking and ringing for candy down their street and over a block before Davy spotted him. Tony was shaking down a younger kid for his candy, pouring the

115

diminutive cowboy's bag of loot into his own. Too mature to be bothered to wear a costume, the fifteen-year-old DeMarco wore his older brother's high school graduation gown and a Red Sox baseball cap.

"Hey Fagula, what's in the box?" Tony had recognized him even under the makeup.

"None of your business, Tony." Davy knew this would anger the larger boy and bring him in close. Tony walked up and grabbed him by the ribbon holding the medal, jerking him forward.

"Listen you little shit, when I ask you a question, you better gimme an answer. Capisce?" He shook Davy and grabbed the twine holding the box from Davy's hand then tossed him backwards, where he fell onto the soft grass of a neighbor's lawn. Eric looked on awkwardly, not sure what to do. To intervene would profusely illustrate how UN-super he really was. He looked at Davy on the ground, his eyes pleading for instruction. Dracula looked up at chubby, unsure Superman. "Run" he said.

Superman ran.

Tony shook the heavy box. It rattled ominously.

"Do NOT open that." Davy told him, knowing he would now have no choice but to open it.

DeMarco smirked at him and pulled the twine, releasing the knot that held the box closed. "Screw that, I wanna know…"

The second the flaps parted, hornets began to pour out of the box, angry at their imprisonment, angry at being shaken, angry at being hornets. Every one of them flew onto Tony DeMarco and stung him. Davy got up and ran to a safer distance, then turned to watch.

"I told you not to open it, you fucking idiot!" he shouted, smiling. The nest had fallen out of the box, hit the sidewalk and broken open releasing even more hornets that lighted on the flailing bully. Davy saw several fly into the armholes of the graduation gown, and DeMarco screamed anew. The bully was panicked and in massive pain.

"Help me, they're killing me!" he shouted, trying to swat them away with his hands.

"If I were you, I'd look for a pond to jump into," Davy said. Then he turned, bent down to grab his sack of candy, and walked home.

***

Davy's stepfather walked into the bedroom wearing his costume for the evening; a dark jacket, turtleneck, pants, and hobnailed boots - the uniform of Frankenstein's monster. All he needed now was a mask, the one sitting on his bed in a padded envelope addressed to him from The Captain Company of Murray Hill, NY. It was nice of Davy to help him find the perfect topper for his outfit, he thought. Davy wasn't a bad kid all the time; he just needed discipline and a strong hand to apply it. Just like his mother. He hated having to hit them, but sometimes it was necessary.

He opened the envelope and stared at the mask. It didn't look much like Frankenstein to him, but it sure was ugly. Turning to the mirror, he slipped it over his head. He sat down on the bed. He screamed a latex-muffled scream. He kept screaming until his voice gave out, then he screamed silently.

Outside in the darkened hallway, Davy watched through the partly opened door. Something gray and pasty bubbled out from under the mask.

He smiled.

End

●

We're honored to include D.C. Phillips, the accomplished author of *Frightful Fables*, the tales that leave you screaming for more! He's received praise for his dynamic and darkly ironic style, described as *Flannery O'Connor* meets *Tales from the Crypt*. As a native of Atlanta, Georgia, D.C. cites Southern culture and classic horror as two of his major influences. He tells us, *"I admire the greats who draw inspiration from their surroundings, from the subtle anxieties of suburbia to the creaky halls of a Victorian manor. My favorite authors and artists find the extraordinary in the ordinary, the horror in the mundane."*

●

Eternal Hills
by D.C. Phillips

A misty haze of rain descended on Tanner Bluff. It would lift in about another week, only to be replaced by blinding-cold November sun. The old timers congregated under the faded awning of Murphy's Cafeteria, scoffing at public alarm over global warming. It certainly wasn't getting warmer around here; if anything, it felt colder than it had last year.

A bell dinged, and conversation came to a familiar halt. Dick Kramer craned his neck to survey the car that had pulled into the lot next door. He let out a sigh and stretched his knees before pushing himself to a standing position. "Be right back, boys. Hold the bullshit for a minute."

Georgia Screeches

The old man steeled himself against the chill of the precipitation - he refused to carry an umbrella by principle; he'd suffered worse - and carried his lanky limbs across the paved stretch that separated his favorite restaurant from the adjacent fill station. It was the last of its kind, where an attendant - in this case Mr. Kramer himself - was summoned by a bell to offer service with a smile...of sorts.

"Good afternoon," the driver of the long beige Nova greeted. He cut the engine of the car and offered an apologetic look. "Sorry to drag you over in this weather."

Mr. Kramer grunted in reply. "Primo?"

"Excuse me?" the man scooted forward in his seat.

The man seemed put off by the request for clarification. "Primo. Premium'll do?"

"Oh, uh, yes."

The old man went about his work. The pump squeaked and clunked and the car shook for a brief moment. As fuel churned from one receptacle to another, the young man called from his window. "Say, sir, could you tell me how to get to Eternal Hills from here?"

Dick shuffled around to the driver's side door, considering the question with hands on hips. For a moment, the driver thought the elderly attendant hadn't heard. "That's a ways off the beaten path. You got kin out there?"

"Yes, sir, my grandfather. Chance McCoy. I'm Bertrand, but most people call me Bert." He offered a shy smile.

Dick's eyebrows shrugged, as if to say, *Doesn't ring any bells.* "You're on the right track. Turn right outta here and just keep followin' the county route. 'Bout two miles down you'll come to a fork; the pavement'll continue to the left, but you'll wanna take the dirt road to the right. That's the drive. It'll dead-end at the cemetery."

The gas pump clicked, signaling a full tank.

"Thank you," Bert said, fishing a couple of rumpled bills from the pocket of his pleated khaki pants. "You can keep the change."

***

Dick's directions were spot-on. Just as Bert began to wonder if the old man had been yanking his chain, the dirt path appeared. Mud pooled in ruts around the base of a faded sign that read ETERNAL HILLS and sloshed dramatically under tire. The holy ground lived up to its namesake; the drive split into a veritable ant colony of superficial paths and more corollary tributaries that went nowhere, more often than not. Markers jutted out from the light fog. They were sporadic icebergs that stood in obedient rows as far as the eye could see. As he made his way forward, he observed that no monument in this front section could date back farther than the 1970s; the in-ground plaques and conical urns were indicative of more contemporary trends.

If memory served him correctly, Grandfather should be buried along the outskirts of this phase. He was laid to rest when Bert was only a child, and the more recent wave of graves hadn't yet been dug. Following the natural curvature of the path, he veered toward the right.

How peculiar, Bert mused. At every turn, the sun appeared to be setting along the horizon, dulled to a fuzzy gray by the cloud cover. It seemed to follow him, a gloomy companion. It caused a kind of melancholy to settle over him, but he didn't quite mind, as the feeling wasn't entirely unpleasant.

Huh. He could've sworn he'd seen that flower arrangement already, too - the daffodils with the green tulle. Had he managed to loop around without noticing?

No matter. He'd swing right at the next fork. He was

sure he hadn't taken a right till now. Here the stones were older, with their weather-worn carvings and poetic inscriptions. This zone of the burial ground came complete with the occasional above-ground slab or modest mausoleum with oxidized doors, like set pieces out of a Poe story.

Ah, there was someone up ahead, walking in the same direction that Bert was heading. By the looks of the equipment that encumbered his belt, he must be some kind of groundskeeper.

"Excuse me," Bert called as he cranked down a window and slowed to idle. "How do I get back to the front gate?"

With no sense of urgency, the handyman turned. He stood there, vacant-eyed. A shock of white hair sharpened the contrast of his dark, dull gaze, and a bucket - filled to the brim with underbrush and the remnants of an Easter arrangement - swung slightly from one closed palm. Just as slowly as he'd turned to face Bert, he turned again and ambled on into the distance.

The melancholy Bert felt minutes earlier gave way to a bubbling sense of dread. He would go back now. Offering a silent apology to his grandfather, he decided to backtrack the way he'd come, and that was that. With no turnabout in sight along the narrow path, he threw the car into reverse, stepped on the accelerator before consulting the rear-view mirror...

...and slammed into the mildewed side of an ornate structure he hadn't yet seen. In fact, he hadn't seen anything like it in the cemetery until now. It was one of myriad low, square buildings that now stretched inexplicably in every direction. They were impossibly old - ancient, even - with crumbling homage to nymphs and mythical beings. He had apparently slipped into yet another section of this sprawling tract. Although by now

121

the clouds had begun to dissipate, the sun was not visible; only its orange-red, aura-streaked fingers across the horizon, over this veritable necropolis.

In that moment Betrand knew that, if he managed to find his way out of this place, his mind was irrevocably fractured.

***

Back at the restaurant, the old timers continued shooting the breeze. Dick occupied a rocker on the edge of the porch, nearest the fill station. While he gazed into the distance, the others studied the back of his wrinkled head.

"That boy that come by earlier," Marvin Trice asked, "where 'zackly was he lookin' to go?"

"Eternal Hills," Dick replied.

The group held a moment of silence.

"Who was he lookin' for all the way out there?" Ralph Headley this time.

Dick rocked back almost imperceptibly. "Granddaddy."

"'Spose he'll find him out there."

Dick snickered. "And then some," he said - and launched a glob of tobacco spit from the inside pocket of his jowl.

The only thing missing from these pages is YOU!

Submit your short horror story to one of our upcoming anthologies. Your story must be 2500 words or less and be set in the region of your 2020 Days of the Dead horror convention:

2020 Deadlines:
Georgia................... Jan. 1st
Nevada................... Feb. 20th
Indiana................... June 19th
Carolinas..................Sept. 1st
Illinois......................Oct. 30th

If your story is chosen, you'll be published in a book and you'll receive:

- o Admission for 2 to your region's Days of the Dead show
- o A complimentary printed copy of your book
- o Ability to purchase additional copies for $1.50 above cost
- o A 20% shared royalty with fellow contributors
- o Participation in an author signing at your Days of the Dead
- o A great feeling of accomplishment as a published writer!

Send submissions to: bbsadmin@downward.com, with the subject line: DAYS OF THE DEAD ANTHOLOGY and the Days of the Dead region you're representing in your story: GA, NV, IN, NC/SC, IL.

Leave the fear to your readers! Write!

Made in the USA
Columbia, SC
04 February 2020